Home is whe [barcode] *be.*

D1535536

It was like another wor... ...y... ...d was laid out with container plants, rock formations, and perennials. Just how Nori had imagined a samurai's garden to be.

"It's perfect," she breathed.

Jiji chuckled. "*Domo arigato.* I am pleased you like it."

As Jiji secured the shed, Baba led Nori up the pebble walkway to a house with smooth stucco walls beneath the swooping gables of a blue ceramic-tile roof. "Welcome to our home," she said in gentle, halting English.

Standing in the step-down entryway, Nori could smell an old-house mustiness beneath the peppery straw of the woven tatami mats.

Nori had a room to herself. Against one wall was a recessed platform that almost looked like a shrine except that there was a flower arrangement and another painted scroll there instead of an idol or something. Her window had a thin film over the glass made to look like rice paper. Baba opened one side.

"Here, Nori-*chan.* You can see Jiji's garden."

Nori peered out the window. A little stone pagoda and a collection of bonsai trees surrounded the lily-filled koi pond, complete with a graceful arching footbridge. Under a bent Japanese maple sat a bench where Nori could imagine spending a lot of time just thinking.

"I leave you to privacy," Baba said. "You rest. We eat soon."

Nori sat by the window and rested her chin on the sill. Even though she hadn't wanted to come, Nori felt strangely comfortable here already. Like she'd come home.

S.A.S.S.

Now and Zen

Linda Gerber

speak

An Imprint of Penguin Group (USA) Inc.

Acknowledgments

Special thanks to my Yas and to my online creative support, without whom I would be lost: Marsha Skrypuch, Karen Dyer, Kate Coombs, Polly Capriotti, Jen McAndrews, Barb Aeschliman, Nicole Maggi, Ginger Calem, and Lee Cutler. And to my editor, Angelle, for making it all work. Domo arigato!

SPEAK
Published by the Penguin Group
Penguin Group (USA) Inc., 345 Hudson Street, New York, New York 10014, U.S.A.
Penguin Group (Canada), 90 Eglinton Avenue East, Suite 700, Toronto, Ontario, Canada M4P 2Y3
(a division of Pearson Penguin Canada Inc.)
Penguin Books Ltd, 80 Strand, London WC2R 0RL, England
Penguin Ireland, 25 St Stephen's Green, Dublin 2, Ireland (a division of Penguin Books Ltd)
Penguin Group (Australia), 250 Camberwell Road, Camberwell, Victoria 3124, Australia
(a division of Pearson Australia Group Pty Ltd)
Penguin Group (NZ), Cnr Airborne and Rosedale Roads, Albany, Auckland 1310,
New Zealand (a division of Pearson New Zealand Ltd)
Penguin Books (South Africa) (Pty) Ltd, 24 Sturdee Avenue, Rosebank, Johannesburg 2196,
South Africa

Registered Offices: Penguin Books Ltd, 80 Strand, London WC2R 0RL, England

Published by Speak, an imprint of Penguin Group (USA) Inc., 2006

1 3 5 7 9 10 8 6 4 2

Interior art and design by Jeanine Henderson. Text set in Imago Book.

LIBRARY OF CONGRESS CATALOGING-IN-PUBLICATION DATA

Gerber, Linda C.
Now and Zen / by Linda Gerber.
p. cm. – (S.A.S.S.: Students Across the Seven Seas)
Summary: American teenager Nori Tanaka has never thought much about her Japanese heritage, but when she travels to Japan for a summer academic program to escape from her parents' impending divorce, she discovers a new way of looking at both herself and the world.
ISBN 0-14-2400657-0 (pbk.)
[1. Foreign study—Fiction. 2. Self-perception—Fiction. 3. Identity—Fiction. 4. Family problems—Fiction. 5. Schools—Fiction. 6. Japan—Fiction.] I. Title. II. Series.
PZ7.G293567Now 2006 [Fic]—dc22 2006042279

Printed in the United States of America

To my family. Thanks for believing.

Tokyo Metropolitan
Government Building

Shinjuku

Hachiko Square

Application for the Students Across the Seven Seas
Study Abroad Program

Name: Noreli Tanaka
Age: 16
High School: Olentangy High School
Hometown: Powell, Ohio
Preferred Study Abroad Destination: Tokyo, Japan

1. Why are you interested in traveling abroad next year?

Answer: I want to make a difference in the world and I believe that the leadership skills I would gain by participating in the Global Outreach program would prepare me to take the reins and lead my generation to a better tomorrow.

(Truth: I don't really care where I go, just as long as I can get away. My parents are making me crazy!)

2. How will studying abroad further develop your talents and interests?

Answer: I hope to attain a global perspective on the social, political and economic issues facing countries outside my own in order to achieve a better understanding of the resulting environmental impact to our world.

(Truth: Me getting out of the house for the summer might just give my mom and dad the space they need to reconnect. Plus I could do my own thing without every move being scrutinized and analyzed and argued about endlessly.)

3. Describe your extracurricular activities.

Answer: At school, I serve as the Student Body Secretary and am the leader of the local chapter of Global Green. I also support the Sierra Club, the Audubon Society and the National Geographic Society.

(Truth: My best friend Val thinks I should be adding more social activities (read: dates) to the line-up and I'm beginning to think she's right.)

4. Is there anything else you feel we should know about you?

Answer: As a Japanese-American, I am eager to connect with my heritage and to learn more about my ancestors by immersing myself in the unique culture of Japan.

(Truth:. . . just as long as my mom keeps her nose out of it and lets me make my own connections!)

Chapter One

Seventeen hours. That's how long it takes to fly from Columbus, Ohio, to Narita, Japan, when you make three stops along the way. Seventeen long hours stuck on a plane with a bunch of losers. Not exactly the experience Nori had envisioned when she signed up for a summer abroad.

This was the first time SASS—Students Across the Seven Seas—had sent students to the Global Outreach program, and from what Nori had seen, it might well be the last. Outreach students were supposed to spend this term in Japan learning the leadership skills necessary to combat global challenges. If her traveling companions were the

leaders of the next generation, the world was in trouble.

There were six in their group: Nori, one other girl, and four completely dorky boys. Not dorky-looking, necessarily; the tall blond from New York and the football captain from Atlanta were actually kinda cute. But looks don't count much when you're throwing food or trying to slap the backs of one another's heads.

She shook the remnants of trail mix from her long, straight, black hair and shot a glare at the boy in the window seat. He just grinned and flipped a peanut past her face at the guy seated in the aisle. The flight attendant had to ask them all to settle down. Nori was so embarrassed she wanted to rip the Global Outreach logo from her blazer and crawl under the seat.

Touchdown in Tokyo didn't come nearly soon enough. The moment she got off the plane, Nori shrugged out of her blazer, stuffed it into her backpack, and lost herself in the crowd at the passport checkpoint. Her freedom was short-lived, however; their escort herded the group back together, and she was stuck with them once more.

At the baggage claim area, Nori perched on one of the padded chairs and watched the other students gather around the carousel. The guys were all showing off for the other girl, Amberly Bryson, and she was eating it up—giggling and fingering her blond curls. Nori shuddered and looked down at the single entry in her travel journal. "The Tokyo-Narita airport is very clean." She didn't have the stomach to write anything more.

"Nori! Come get in the picture!" Amberly waved like she was bringing in a plane. She'd arranged the dork squad in front of a sign written in kanji characters that probably said something like FOOLISH AMERICANS MAY STAND HERE FOR PHOTOGRAPHS.

Nori shook her head. No way.

"Come on, Nori," Amberly persisted. "It will be a memory!"

"That's what I'm afraid of."

The carousel lurched into motion before Amberly could say anything further. The guys drifted from their appointed positions, eyes fixed on the suitcases dropping from the chute.

Amberly's smile faltered, but that didn't stop her from joining them. "Grab mine if you see it," she said. "Blue floral with a big pink bow on the handle."

Nori rolled her eyes. Why am I not surprised?

After clearing customs, the group rolled their suitcases through the sliding doors into the crowded arrival lobby, where a tall Japanese man carrying a hand-lettered Global Outreach sign rushed forward to greet them. He bowed deeply.

"*Yokoso!*" he said. "Welcome. My name is Koske Wada,

but you can call me Wada-*sensei*." His dark eyes crinkled at the edges as he gave them a broad smile.

Nori eyed him with approval. The information packet she'd received with her registration materials had explained the use of honorific titles like *san* or *chan* or *kun*. You tacked them onto people's names to show respect. *Sensei* was a title that meant master or teacher. As teachers went, Wada-*sensei* looked pretty cool. He had a casual air about him from his Daniel Radcliffe hair to his rumpled khakis and Teva sandals. Not that it had anything to do with cool, but his English was perfect. Not even a trace of an accent. She was impressed.

He consulted his clipboard and called out their names one by one, pausing for an affirmative "here." Satisfied, he nodded. "Right. Now let's get a move on. The other groups are already loading on the bus. Yours was the last flight in."

They quickly exchanged their dollars for yen and stopped by a kiosk to get snacks for the long ride to Tokyo.

"Oh, look at this!" Amberly held up a packet of stiff alien-looking things. "Dried squid!"

Nori grimaced and put down the rice crackers she'd been holding. That did it. Killed the appetite. If there was one thing in the world she absolutely couldn't stomach, it was fish. She grabbed a bottle of water and headed to the counter.

A postcard display caught her eye. She'd promised her mom and dad that she would write as soon as she got to Tokyo. Separate cards, of course. A wave of sadness threatened, and she pushed it away. No. No thinking about them. This trip was about getting away from their troubles, not bringing them with her. She grabbed a couple of random postcards and hurried to the checkout counter.

By the time Nori's small group got to the bus, everyone else had already boarded. Nori slid into the first free row she could find and dropped her backpack onto the empty seat beside her. She started up her iPod and stared out the window, trying not to notice Amberly standing expectantly in the aisle.

Amberly reached for the backpack. "Would you like me to put this in the overhead?"

Nori sighed. "No, that's okay." She pulled it onto her lap, and Amberly slid into the empty seat.

As the bus rolled slowly through the evening traffic, Nori tried without much success to write to her parents. After about an hour of intense concentration, all she had come up with was "Dear Dad, I'm here." The letters looked like a first-grader had scribbled them because each time the bus bumped or swayed, her hand bumped or swayed with it. She rubbed her eyes and tried to focus on the card, but in the shadows, the words became a blur. Yawning, she looked around the bus. Most everyone else appeared to be asleep— and no wonder. It was like five in the morning back home.

She tucked the cards into her backpack and leaned her head against the back of the seat, letting her heavy eyelids drift shut.

Amberly suddenly bounced up and down in her seat, shaking Nori's shoulder. "Look!" she squealed. "Isn't that cool?"

"Wha—?" Nori opened one eye just a crack.

"The Rainbow Bridge!" She leaned over Nori to look out the window. Up ahead was the suspension bridge that spanned part of Tokyo Bay. Nori had read about it in the information packet. It had been designed so that the white towers would harmonize with the Tokyo Harbor. Nori had liked that word, *harmonize*, imagining Japan as a utopia of cherry blossoms, swoopy rooftops, and serenity.

She craned her neck to see the bridge ahead. Green, white, and red solar-powered lights illuminated the two towers of the bridge, just like the information packet had described. Nori might have been impressed if she hadn't been so tired.

"Oh, and look at the Ferris wheel!" Amberly twisted in her seat and pointed out the windows on the other side of the bus to where a huge Ferris wheel striped in neon lights slowly circled. "I hope we can ride that while we're here. It's like the biggest in the world. You're supposed to be able to see for miles at the top. Or should I say, for kilometers?" She giggled.

"Mmm-hmmm." Nori tried to close her eyes once more, but Amberly continued to shake her arm.

"Oh. My. Gosh. Have you seen anything so cool in your life?" They were on the Rainbow Bridge now, crawling along in traffic, and to the right lay Tokyo, which, Nori had to admit, was pretty impressive. Black silhouettes of buildings stood stark against a twilight purple sky, the lights in their windows like a galaxy of stars, all reflected in the water of the bay.

"It must be like coming home for you, huh?"

"What are you talking about?"

"You know, being Japanese. This must be such an awesome experience for you."

Nori clenched her jaw. *Give me a break.* "I'm not Japanese. I'm American."

"Oh. I meant…"Amberly's voice raised an octave. "Well, you have such Japanese features, and—"

"Slanted eyes don't make a person Japanese, Amberly."

"But…isn't Tanaka a Japanese name?"

Nori shot her a look. "Yeah. Just like Bryson is a British name. Does that make you English?"

Amberly twisted a strand of golden honey hair around her French-manicured finger. "Actually, I'm Welsh and Scottish and Danish, and if you go back far enough—"

Nori held up a hand. "The answer to your question is no. It isn't like coming home for me because I've never been to Japan before." What she didn't say was that she was here now only to get away from her parents' fighting. She would just as happily have gone to Timbuktu.

She folded her arms, hunched down in her seat, and squinched her eyes shut, even though now she was much too irritated to sleep.

Amberly must have caught her mood because she

backed off. "There's Tokyo Tower," she murmured, but she left Nori's arm alone.

Nori looked out the window of the bus as they pulled in front of the dorm building, surprised to see that it wasn't located near a campus at all, but in the middle of a long block of businesses and shops. She gathered her things and followed the others through the sliding-glass doors into the lobby, which, with its low couches and tables, looked more like an oversize dentist's office waiting room than a place for students to gather. Not that Nori really cared. She was so tired all she could think about was a shower and a bed.

That is, until Wada-*sensei* handed out the room assignments.

Amberly squealed and hugged Nori. "Roommates! We're going to have so much fun! I just know it." She grabbed the key. "Come on!"

Grinding her teeth, Nori bent to pick up her backpack. The front doors slid open, and she glanced up. Her breath caught. Striding into the lobby was a tall, blond, broad-shouldered hottie who looked just like Orlando Bloom, only cuter. She smiled. This summer just might be more interesting than she'd thought.

Nori rose with the sun, which was not such a good thing since in Japan in June the sun makes its appearance at about four A.M. Actually, she'd been awake for a long time, and her head ached from trying to force herself to go back to sleep.

Amberly, of course, had no such problem and was snoring daintily in her frou-frou pink pajamas and matching satin eye mask.

Nori suppressed a shudder and set about folding up her blankets and futon. She stacked them neatly in the closet and slid the screen shut. Now what? Breakfast was not for another three hours.

She turned slowly, taking in the shadowy confines of their small dorm room. Wasn't much to see, really. Just the futons and two low tables that would serve as desks for the next seven weeks. A series of sliding screens along one wall concealed closets and shelves, and a sliding-glass door on another led out to a narrow balcony. The other walls were completely blank. Drab. Blah.

Suddenly feeling very claustrophobic, Nori stepped over Amberly and let herself outside onto the balcony. The streets below were quiet and dreary in the early morning light. A red paper lantern hung in the doorway of the business across the street, but that was the only breath of color among the boxy gray buildings as far as she could see.

A movement below caught her attention, and she looked down to see a lone black cat limp across the street. Nori leaned over the railing and watched until the cat disappeared into a dark alleyway. For some reason she couldn't

quite grasp, the sight of the solitary cat made her sad.

She turned abruptly and went inside. "Get a grip, Tanaka," she muttered.

Amberly's voice echoed in her head, *Isn't Tanaka a Japanese name?*

Truth was, Nori didn't know how to *be* Japanese. She could remember little things from when she lived near her grandparents in San Francisco: how to say "good morning" and "good night," how to eat with chopsticks, how to fold paper into little bird shapes. But most of her life she'd lived in Ohio, far away from such memories. Her parents had never much cared to carry on the traditions. They were too busy trying be like everybody else. Maybe that's why they couldn't get along anymore. They'd lost themselves along the way.

Nori sighed. She wasn't supposed to be thinking about them. She was supposed to be starting an adventure.

Grabbing her toiletry bag from the closet, she padded down the cool tile hallway to the community bathroom. At least there was one advantage to being up so early; it wouldn't be crowded there yet. She took her time getting ready, and before long she felt like herself again, parents and melancholy at least temporarily forgotten.

Here I am, sitting in the lobby of our dorm, waiting for the day to start.

Breakfast this morning was barbecued eel and rice. Ate the rice.

Found out who the blond guy is. His name is Erik Sussmann, and he's from Germany. I heard he signed up for ecology. A fellow environmentalist. I think I'm in love. Hope he's in my class!

Also hope they don't make us wear these stupid navy blazers everywhere. It's already a sauna outside at only eight in the morning.

"Konnichiwa!" Amberly slid onto the padded bench beside Nori.

Nori slapped her journal shut and forced a smile. "I think it's *ohayo gozaimasu,*" she said. *"Konnichiwa* is for afternoon."

Amberly giggled. "You're right. Isn't it funny that 'Ohio' means 'good morning'?"

Rolling her eyes, Nori slipped her journal into her backpack. "Hysterical."

Amberly crossed her tanned legs, bouncing one foot. She twisted a strand of hair around her finger as she scanned the crowded lobby. "So, are you ready for this?"

"For what?"

"This. Different culture, killer courses. Nothing but AP classes! My friends at home thought I was crazy to want to spend my summer doing schoolwork, but I really needed something to pad my résumé for college, you know?" She turned to Nori, eyes bright. "How about you? Why'd you want to take this on?"

Nori shifted in her seat. "Oh, you know. That whole save-the-world thing."

Amberly giggled. "Yeah, that, too." She quieted for a moment, shifting gears. "Wonder who I'll get paired with today? Wouldn't it be fun if you and I could be partners?"

Nori's smile froze. "Uh—"

Just in time, the director, Ms. Jameson, clapped her hands and yelled, "Listen up, people!" Not like she even needed to raise her voice; if she just walked into a room, her height alone commanded attention. She must have been nearly six feet tall, with an athletic build that spoke of years on the basketball court. Her short-cropped gray hair might have looked totally butch if it wasn't for the way she gelled it in upturned spikes, accenting her high cheekbones.

She waited for the buzz of conversation to die down before she held up a copy of the Tokyo Railway train map. "We are about to venture out on one of the busiest transit systems in the world, and we don't want to lose anyone. If you get separated from the group, the route is clearly marked on the map. The opening ceremony begins promptly at nine o'clock, and we will not accept getting lost as a valid excuse for tardiness."

A murmur rose from the group, accompanied by a rustling of paper as train maps were withdrawn from folders. Ms. Jameson clapped her hands again.

"People! Pay attention! As I call your name and your partner's name, please exit together through the door on your left. Our local students will lead you to the station and help you purchase your tickets." The lobby fell silent, and she cleared her throat. "Aalto, Kirsti and Annunzio, Pasqualle... Atherton, Josef and Ayala, Luis..."

"She's doing it alphabetically," Amberly whispered.

Nori rolled her eyes and nodded, but quickly fished in her backpack for her packet. She thumbed through it until she found the student list. Running her finger down the page, she read, Patterson, Skinner, Sussmann, Tanaka... Yes! There was a God! She hugged the paper and waited for her name to be called along with Erik's.

Amberly was paired with a girl from the Philippines. Nori watched through the window as they left, Amberly clutching at the girl's arm, yammering the moment they stepped out the door. Nori raised a fist in solidarity with the poor girl. Hang in there, sister.

After what seemed like a very long time, Ms. Jameson reached the *S*'s. "Sussmann, Erik and..."

Nori stood.

"Thompson, James."

What? No! Face burning, Nori slumped into her seat and watched her dream partner exchange introductory grunts with the Atlanta football bonehead. She hardly paid attention to the rest of the names being read until she realized she was the last person left.

"Uh, Ms. Jameson?"

The director furrowed her brow and glanced down at Nori's name tag. "Miss Tanaka? Is everything under control?"

"Yeah. But I don't have a partner."

"We didn't assign partners to locals," she said in a tone fit for a three-year-old. "You're supposed to be assisting the others."

"But I'm not local." Duh. Look at the little American flag on my lapel.

"Oh, dear. Well, you'll have to come with me. We can figure it out after we get settled."

They caught the rest of the group as they lined up to buy tickets outside Shinjuku station. Ms. Jameson hurried off to herd the students through the electronic turnstiles while Nori fought her way toward the ticket machine.

She had never seen so many people in one place in her life—every one of them in a hurry. Nori watched carefully as the people ahead of her rapidly fed yen coins into boxy machines and pushed buttons. Looked easy enough.

Wrong.

She tried several times, but the machine kept beeping at her. Finally, a Japanese kid no older than ten stepped forward to help. He gave her a look that clearly said she should know how to do this. By the time she made it through the turnstile, she couldn't see anyone from her group.

Fighting panic, she checked the map. The Yamanote Line.

Track twelve. And thirteen. Which one? People bumped into her as they rushed past. So much for polite.

Up ahead, Nori caught a glimpse of curly, blond hair amid the sea of black. Yes! She fought her way into the stream of commuters heading to track thirteen. It wasn't easy, but she finally made it to the crowded platform. The blond girl turned her head. It was not Amberly.

Nori spun around. Nothing but black suits and briefcases, school uniforms and backpacks.

A train pulled away.

There was her group, on the opposite platform—track number twelve. She pushed her way back up the stairs and fought against the tide of commuters to reach them.

Nori arrived at the correct platform about the same time as the train. Its doors slid open, and a mass of people spilled out. Again she was jostled and pushed back. Her group started to board the train.

"Excuse me. *Sumimasen. Sumima*—"Oh, what the heck. "MOVE!" She lowered a shoulder and plowed through the crowd. By the time she reached the train it was full to over-flowing. Literally. Some people looked like they were going to fall out of the doors. But that didn't stop more from trying to force their way on board. Uniformed men with white gloves helped to push them in.

Just in front of Nori, a dainty Japanese woman in a con-servative business suit and pumps pushed like a linebacker

until she wedged herself into the nucleus of passengers. If she could do it, Nori could, too.

She removed her backpack and held it in front of her like a battering ram as she struggled forward. A gloved hand shoved from behind. She got one foot inside the door.

A bell chimed.

The hand now grabbed her shoulder and pulled her back as the doors slid closed...right onto her backpack. She lost her grip. The train rolled away.

It happened so fast that all Nori could do was watch helplessly as the train picked up speed.

Great. Just great. She might be at the right platform. She might know the correct train to take. But her map was in her backpack and her backpack was on that train and she had no idea which stop was hers.

Her first day in Tokyo and she was lost.

Chapter Two

In fourth grade, Nori had gone camping with the Girl Scouts. During a hike in the woods, she somehow got separated from her troop. She'd had the same helpless, edge-of-panic sensation then that she was feeling now. Only she wasn't ten years old anymore, and this totally wasn't Girl Scouts.

She bit her lip to quell the barb of panic twisting in her stomach. How was she going to find her group? What if someone took her backpack? She'd read that theft was not a big problem in Japan's honor-driven society, but what if someone forgot to be honorable? All her stuff was in that backpack—iPod, wallet, ID, school packet, travel journal.

A man with a briefcase bumped past her and took his place on the platform. People were already lining up for the next train. She could get on this one easily. But then what?

When she was a Girl Scout, she'd been instructed to hug a tree if she ever got lost and to stay put until someone came to find her. The same logic applied now—only not the tree-hugging part.

She stood by a signpost and waited.

And waited.

The airless platform grew hotter by the minute. She peeled off her blazer and fanned herself with a sleeve, watching people cram into the train cars. Each train grew successively less crowded as rush hour waned.

More waiting as she shifted her weight from one foot to the other. She twisted her long hair up and fanned her neck, starting to have second thoughts. This is stupid. No one is coming. Maybe I should just try to find my way back to the dorms, where at least it's cool and I can sit down and—

"Nori-*san*?"

She jumped and spun around to find a lanky Japanese boy in an Outreach blazer standing before her. He was cute in a surfer-boy kind of way; shaggy hair bleached on the ends, casual posture, awesome build, easy grin. She smiled in return.

"Atsushi Shiota at your service," he said. "I think this belongs to you." With a bow, he held out her backpack with both hands.

Gathering it into her arms, she bowed as well. "Thank you! *Domo arigato*."

"*Daijobu, daijobu*. It's okay." He waved her thanks away. "I saw you get left behind, so I jumped off at the next station and came back." He cocked his head to the side. "I might have found you easier if you had your jacket on. You kind of blend in, you know?"

Nori fingered her black hair and smiled sheepishly. "It was hot."

"It's only June. You should feel it in August."

"No, thank you."

He laughed. "Wimp."

"Hey, seven weeks of this will be more than enough."

"You get used to it."

"So you're from here? You speak English really well."

He bowed just a little, dark eyes bright. "Yeah, I lived in the States for a while."

"Ah. That explains it. Where?"

"Ohio. Lived there for five years."

"Get out! I'm from Ohio."

"Where?"

"Powell. Near Columbus."

"Sure, I know where that is. We were in Dublin. My dad works for Honda."

She raised her brows.

"Hey, I know what you're thinking, but he's with an environmentally friendly automaker."

"Wha–?"

"You're taking the course on the Kyoto Accord, right?"

"Yeah, but how did you...?"

He nodded at her backpack. "I had to find out your name to tell the counselors who I was going after. Hope you don't mind."

"No, no. That's okay." But she could feel the heat rising in her face. *Please don't say you looked in my journal.*

He smiled as if he could read her thoughts and gestured with his chin. "This is our train. Let's go."

By the time Nori and Atsushi reached the International School compound, the opening ceremony had already begun. Good thing Atsushi knew his way around; Nori was sure she would have gotten lost trying to find the campus auditorium. The compound included not only the high school where the Outreach classes would be held, but a middle school and an elementary school as well, all surrounding a large, tree-filled courtyard. But even with him leading the way, they were late.

"Don't worry about it," Atsushi whispered as they slipped into the darkened auditorium.

Nori stood for a moment to let her eyes adjust. On the stage sat several adults who Nori could only guess were the faculty. She recognized Wada-*sensei* and Ms. Jameson, who was just stepping up to the podium.

Atsushi quickly guided Nori to an empty seat.

Ms. Jameson banged a gavel. "I hereby declare this session of Global Outreach officially open. We are thrilled to be able to meet in Japan this year and would like to thank our local coordinators for their hard work and dedication in bringing this together."

She paused for the students to applaud.

"Would our local students please stand?" Nearly a quarter of the participants rose to their feet. "These students have already given graciously of their time and energy to arrange host families for all of your home visits in Tokyo, to consult on field trips, and to organize class outings."

More applause.

She droned on about rules and regulations. Nori yawned, the lack of sleep catching up to her. Only half listening, she rested her chin on her hand and closed her eyes.

"Please check your schedules carefully," Ms. Jameson said. "You will have two classes on A day and two on B day. Make a note of the rotation."

Blah, blah, blah. All this stuff was in the registration materials. Nori already knew that she had study hall each morning, followed by international economics and history of Japan on A days and world ecology and Japanese culture on B days. She knew that afternoons and Sundays would be spent sightseeing as a group, and Saturdays were personal days for preparation and such. The packet already described

the two overnight field trips during the term as well as the home-stay visits, where students each would get to see what it was like to live with a Japanese family for a week. Why rehash everything? She'd rather sleep.

And she almost did, until Ms. Jameson's voice rose several decibels. "And we are pleased to announce a special incentive this year. One outstanding student will be awarded the newly established Global Outreach scholarship, in the amount equivalent to fifteen thousand U.S. dollars, to promote your continued study of global issues."

A buzz of excitement rose among the students. Nori bolted upright, wide awake now.

"People. People." Ms. Jameson banged the gavel again and waited until everyone quieted down before she spoke again. "This scholarship will go to the student who most embodies the spirit of insight and inspiration needed to bring together the different cultures of our changing world. Both your in-class grades and your Global Outreach Summit presentation at the end of the term will be considered in judging the scholarship winner."

Nori's mind raced. The presentations were supposed to be independent projects, based on things learned at the conference, that would somehow impact the world for good. Her devotion to ecology would definitely work in her favor. She could focus on climate change or emissions trading or something like that. She already knew a lot about those.

Glancing around, she could see aggressiveness in the

eyes of several students around her. Competition for the scholarship would be fierce.

Nori bent over her desk, scowling as she slogged through a chapter on international trade theory for economics. It didn't seem fair to have homework on the first day. She glanced at her computer screen, mentally calculating the time difference between Tokyo and Ohio. It was nearly seven in the morning at home. Her best friend, Val, would be leaving for school in less than a half hour. If she didn't sign on soon there was no way—

Val's icon lit up, accompanied by an electronic knocking.

Valerivalera: NE1 home?

Nori grinned and slapped her textbook shut.

Revengelobster: Thought you would never show up

Valerivalera: UR so impatient. So how's it goin?

Revengelobster: Already have homework

Valerivalera: Bummr? What's it like?

Revengelobster: Homework?

Valerivalera: Ha ha. School

Revengelobster: Wild. Never felt so outnumbered B4. Ovr 80 students & only 7 American. Am only 1 in some classes.

"Nori?"

Nori jumped. She hadn't even heard Amberly come back into the room.

Revengelobster: BRB
Valerivalera: K

"Yeah?" She twisted in her chair to see Amberly holding a folded piece of paper as if it might explode.

"It's from Ms. Jameson," she said in a hushed voice. "You're supposed to go to the office right away."

Nori's heart dropped. Probably going to get reprimanded for being late that morning. She sighed.

Revengelobster: G2G ☹
Valerivalera: WAAAAH. TTYL
Revengelobster: TTFN

"You wanted to see me?" Nori swung through the dorm's office door to find Ms. Jameson on the phone. "Oh, I'm sorry."

She started to back out, but Ms. Jameson shook her head and gestured for Nori to stay. "That will be just fine," she was saying. "She's here now. I'll let you tell her yourself." She placed her hand over the receiver and held it out to Nori. "It's your mother," she whispered.

Nori's stomach tightened. What would make her penny-pinching mom call overseas? "Is everything all right?"

Ms. Jameson gave her a patronizing smile. "Of course it is." She nodded at the phone. "Take it."

Nori accepted the receiver hesitantly. "Hello?"

"Nori! Sweetie! How are you enjoying Japan?"

"It's okay."

"Just okay? How did your first day go?"

"Fine." Nori worried the telephone cord in her fingers. "What's going on?"

"I have fabulous news for you. Remember when we talked about your great-aunt and uncle who live in Kyoto? Well, we've been able to arrange for your home stay to be spent at their house. Isn't that wonderful?"

Nori blanched. She lowered her voice, turning her back to Ms. Jameson's inquisitive eyes. "I thought we decided we wouldn't do that."

"Well, we weren't sure we could, but the organizers have been kind enough to—"

"But I don't know them, Mom."

"That's the entire point, sweetie. What better chance to get to know them than to spend some time with them?"

Nori ground her teeth. Trust Mom to pull something like this when she knew the director was within earshot and Nori wouldn't make a scene. She cupped her hand over the receiver. "Why are you doing this?"

"Why, sweetheart, I thought you'd be pleased."

"Pleased? We talked about it at home! I said I didn't want—"

Her mother's voice tightened. "You're just nervous."

"Don't tell me what I am."

"Do not take that tone with me, Noreli."

Nori bit her lip. This was so unfair. Everyone else would be staying with families in Tokyo. They'd probably see one another during the week. She would totally miss out. "I would rather stay here."

"You'll feel different about it when you meet them. They are such lovely people."

"But I don't speak the language. Everyone seems to think I should, but I don't. What am I supposed to talk about, sushi and wasabi? That's about all I know, Mom."

"Oh, relax, honey. Your uncle Kentaro speaks perfect English. Besides, you would have had a language challenge no matter who you stayed with."

"But—"

"It's been decided, Nori. And I hope you will be more gracious to them and to your school administrators than you have just been with me."

"But I—"

"Oh, dear. Look at the time. I need to get to work, sweetheart. Have fun! I love you."

Nori dug the toe of her sandal into the carpet. "Love you, too."

Her mother made an annoying kissing noise and hung up. Nori stood for a moment to gather her composure, then turned to replace the phone on the hook.

Ms. Jameson smiled cheerily, green eyes bright with curiosity. "So everything's settled?"

Nori pasted on a smile of her own. "Yes, ma'am," she said. "My mother has taken care of everything."

Just like always.

Chapter Three

Today sucks. I'm only halfway through with it, but I think that's a pretty accurate assessment. It's only the second day of school, but I'm ready to go home. Well, maybe not home, but far away from here.

Where to start? Maybe with Mr. Chivalry. Atsushi is a really nice guy and all, but it's like he thinks he's obligated to follow some samurai Bushido code of honor or something; he saved me, so now he's responsible for me. Everywhere I turn, there he is.

Walked me to the train this morning, and I could tell his friend didn't think that was cool. Japanese girl named Michiko. Atsushi told me Michi means righteous and Ko means child, so the name fits— she's a self-righteous baby. Real snooty. You should have seen the look she gave me when she realized I didn't speak Japanese.

She's about the only one who seems to have picked up on that, though. Everyone else assumes I'm native, and they speak English to me real s-l-o-w. Or loud. Either way, it's very annoying.

Nori chewed on the end of her pen as she reread the entry. That last bit, she had to admit, was kind of her own fault. The assumption could easily be corrected, but for some reason she didn't make the effort. Maybe her experience in ecology class had something to do with it. She shuddered at the memory.

There she was, minding her own business, coloring in all the *O*'s on the course handout, when Nakamura-*sensei* asked, "Isn't that right, Miss Tanaka?"

She'd looked up, totally lost. "Huh?"

He raised a brow, giving her a steely look. "In the face of global threats to the environment, our only hope is international cooperation. Would you agree?"

"Oh. Yes. Absolutely."

"It will never happen," blurted a zit-faced guy in the back row. "Not as long as we have arrogant superpowers who care only for their own welfare."

The girl next to him nodded. "Yes. Like the U.S.A., hogging resources and spitting out pollution."

"They're not the only ones," another girl countered. "What about China and India? They're not even required to meet the same standards as other industrialized nations under the Kyoto Accord. And if China meets their projection of ten million more cars in the next decade—"

"Oh, come on," said Zit-boy. "The United States pumps out more CO_2 than the rest of the world combined. But they don't care as long as the big corporations get what they want and everyone can drive around in their SUVs. Why do you think the Americans didn't sign on to the accord in the first place? It's all about money and power."

The debate continued, but the gist of it was that America was the Great Satan and all the world's woes could be traced back to U.S. carelessness and conspicuous consumption.

Nori sank down in her chair, quietly slipped the American flag pin from her lapel, and hid it in her pocket.

Meanwhile, Nakamura-*sensei* did nothing to stop the America-bashing. In fact, he seemed to agree with the comments being tossed about. Finally, he redirected the class's attention.

"It would appear that we are aware of the problems," he said, perching on the edge of his desk. "What we need to focus on in this class are solutions." He held up a piece of paper. "For example, this is from an essay written by one of your fellow students that shows real promise. It is exactly the sort of thinking I want you all to strive for." Clearing his throat dramatically, he began to read.

"'Simple answers to even the most complex problems are staring us in the face. Take greenhouse gases and the resulting global warming, for example. Scientific studies conclude that doubling the green area on the earth's surface will not only put an end to global warming, but would stabilize climate extremes, absorb pollution, and purify groundwater.

"'Reforestation is the answer. Trees can absorb as much as seven hundred fifty tons of carbon per square kilometer per year.'"

The bell rang. Nakamura-*sensei* laid the papers on his desk and raised his voice above the postclass buzz. "Solutions, class. Let's be looking for solutions."

Nori stood, slowly zipping her backpack, the words of the essay echoing in her head. It was like having her own thoughts read aloud from that paper. She was a huge proponent of reforestation. She'd even led tree-planting drives at her school. As she passed Nakamura-*sensei*'s desk, she nudged the paper around so that she could read the title.

"Practical Solutions to Global Challenges," by Erik Sussmann.

A smile tugged at her lips as a warm tingle rippled through her. Ah. A man with looks *and* brains. She was so totally in love.

Atsushi, of course, had found Nori after class and had shown her the best spot to eat lunch—in the courtyard, under the shade of an acacia tree. She was sitting there now, trying to think of something else to write in her journal. She finally gave up and contented herself with just sitting and watching the lunchtime circus while Atsushi went to get the food.

"You save the spot, and I'll grab lunch," he'd said. Even if she was bugged by his chivalry act, she didn't turn down the offer. The day was hot, and the line at the kiosk was long.

She'd watched as he strode across the lawn, admiring the confidence in his step, the squareness of his shoulders. He was one of those guys who drew you to them just by the way they carried themselves. Plus the fact that he was about a nine on the Hotness Scale. Lean, athletic build; easy smile; tousled hair that only those kinds of guys can pull off. Too bad he was just hanging out with her out of obligation.

But then again, she had decided to go after Erik Sussmann, so what did it matter?

"This seat taken?" Nori squinted up at a tall girl with fiery red hair and a sprinkling of freckles who pointed to the opposite bench.

"No. Feel free."

The girl's smile broadened as she extended her hand. "Name's Kiah, from Oz, Sydney to be specific. Thanks a bunch...uh..."

"Nori." She shook Kiah's hand.

"Pleased to meet ya, Nori. Your English is ace. You been studying long?" She wrestled with the tab on a can of Coke.

"Actually—"

Kiah's soda exploded, spraying in all directions, and she leaped from her seat. "Oh, bloody oath!" She held the can at arm's length, laughing. "That'll teach me, eh?" She took a sip. "How 'bout you? You eating or what?"

"Yeah. My friend's getting the food." Nori shaded her eyes and scanned the line until she saw Atsushi, still twelve people back from the register. She hoped he hadn't chosen anything too starchy. Seriously. Rice and noodles had been the staple of every meal since she'd arrived. What she wanted to know was how everyone in Japan was so skinny when they took in so many carbs. If she kept eating like that, she'd blow up like a carnival balloon.

Amberly walked into view, looking like a Gap model in her khaki walking shorts and sleeveless white cotton shirt, blazer slung carelessly over one shoulder. Two Japanese boys trailed behind her like obedient puppy dogs, one carrying her books and the other a lunch tray. Amberly spotted Nori, waved, and directed her devotees toward the acacia tree.

Kiah raised a brow. "You friends with Blondie?"

"My roommate," Nori said.

"Perky little thing, ain't she?"

"You said it."

Amberly greeted Nori and Kiah and plopped down on the bench, fluttering a painted fan near her face. "Man, it's really hotsui!"

Nori waited for one of the boys to correct her, but they just smiled stupidly. "Um, the word is '*atsui*,'" she said.

"Yeah, like I said." Amberly flapped her collar. "It's hot!"

The boys were still standing, so Nori gestured to a free bench. "Please, have a seat."

They sat.

Awkward silence.

"I'm Nori," she said finally. "Amberly's roommate. This is Kiah, from Australia."

Amberly blushed, which of course just made her look cuter. "Oh! Where are my manners? Nori, this is Yoshi and uh..."

"Teruo."

"Yes, Teruo." She smiled contentedly.

"*Hajimemashite*," Nori said. "Pleased to meet you."

Amberly motioned to Yoshi, and he handed her a clear plastic box containing artfully arranged pieces of sushi. "Look what we did in class. Rolled our own sushi."

Nori forced a smile. "Yum."

Atsushi finally returned, carrying two water bottles and a jumble of food on a tray. He nodded in greeting as introductions were made. "Here you go," he said, handing Nori one of the bottles. "And you have your choice of tuna or salmon *onigiri.*" He offered two green triangular things wrapped in plastic.

Nori recoiled. Not fish! And what was that green stuff? Seaweed? Gag. "Uh...I don't really care. Which do you prefer?"

She ended up with the tuna triangle, a large apple, and a cookie with nasty-looking frosting the color of Pepto-Bismol. At least she could eat the apple.

"So what class do you have next?" Atsushi asked.

"Japanese culture."

"Cool. We have that one together."

Nori blinked. "You're taking culture class? Why?"

"What? You don't think I can be cultured?"

"No," she said. "I mean...why take a class about your own country's culture?"

He shrugged. "It's required. Maybe so we can make sure the gaijins actually learn something."

"Gaijin? What's that?"

"You are. A gaijin is a foreigner."

"Wait," said Kiah. She knit her brows and looked from Atsushi to Nori. "Aren't you from—"

"There you are," a voice cut in. "I have been looking all over for you."

Oh, great. Michiko. As if the day weren't bad enough.

Atsushi squinted up at her. "Well, you found me."

She narrowed her kohl-rimmed eyes. "Did you at least save me a seat?"

"You may sit here," Teruo offered.

Michiko bowed graciously. *"Arigato,"* she purred. "You are very kind."

Teruo about fell over himself moving his books so she could sit. Nori rolled her eyes. Guys are so predictable. Show them anything in a skirt, and they start salivating like Pavlov's dogs. And if the girl happens to have the body of a model, the grace of a dancer, and long, silky tresses that she can toss alluringly over her shoulder, then forget about it. They're gone.

Suddenly self-conscious, Nori fingered her own limp hair.

"Look! I did it!" Amberly proudly held up a piece of sushi with her chopsticks. But then the chopsticks slipped, and the sushi tumbled to the ground. "Oh, poop."

"It requires practice," Yoshi assured her.

"Well, this way is easier." She picked up a new piece with her fingers and squirted it with soy sauce from a little foil packet.

Michiko nudged Teruo and snorted in disgust, but he had refocused his devotion on Amberly, apparently forgetting that it was considered rude in Japan to eat with one's hands. That's what the booklet they got with their registration materials said, anyway. But Teruo just sat there with a goofy smile on his face and didn't say a word. Not even when Amberly licked the dribble of soy sauce that had snaked down her thumb.

"Hey, Nori." She held up another piece of sushi. "You want some?"

"No, thanks."

"Oh! You'll love this!" Amberly peeled the seaweed from around the edge of her sushi. "Guess what they called this in class? 'Nori!' Your name means 'roasted seaweed'! I about died."

Michiko, who had been daintily sipping her Mitsuya Cider, coughed to hide her laughter.

Face burning, Nori stood. "You know what? I have to go."

"Nori…" Atsushi started to stand.

She shook her head and took a step back. "No, don't get up. See you in class, okay? Kiah, it was nice to meet you."

Amberly frowned. "See you after school?"

"Wouldn't miss it." Nori shouldered her backpack and, with a farewell nod to Yoshi, Michiko, and Teruo, she escaped.

Nori was the first to arrive at culture class, and not on purpose, either. After eating her apple in the girls' bathroom, she didn't know where else to go. Feeling totally lame, she took a seat at the far side of the room near the window, pulled out her course outline, and pretended to read.

Before long, more students trickled into the room in twos

or threes, laughing, smiling. Nori watched them over the top of her paper, very conscious of the empty seats remaining around her.

Just when she thought things couldn't possibly get any worse, Michiko walked in with two other girls. Michiko spotted Nori, whispered something behind her hand to her friends, and they all snickered as they took seats at the back of the room.

Nori sank lower in her chair.

"She's a piece of work, that one." Kiah slid behind the desk opposite Nori, eyeing Michiko and company with distaste.

Nori followed her gaze. "You know her, then?"

"Know of her. My mates warned me about her. She's out to win the scholarship any way she can. Her specialty is eliminating the competition—especially the male competition. Like a black widow."

As if she knew they were talking about her, Michiko looked up and shot them a glare so cold that Nori actually shivered. She would have liked to check out of the class right then, but Wada-*sensei* chose that moment to walk in.

The bell rang.

The door closed with a dead thunk.

Nori had just about resigned herself to another horrible class experience when the door opened again.

In strolled Erik Sussmann.

Afternoon sunlight streamed through the windows

behind him, illuminating his hair in golden hues. Nori could almost hear the angelic choir in the background as he paused, striking a heroic pose, navy blazer spanning broad shoulders. He nodded casually to the teacher and scanned the room with cobalt eyes. Her breath caught as those eyes passed over her to the next seat, which was vacant. She straightened, smoothing a hand over her hair, a smile playing on her lips. He took a step toward her. Violins joined in the chorus and…

Screeched to a halt as the door yanked open one more time.

Erik paused midstep and glanced behind him. Atsushi rushed in, breathless. He bowed to Wada-*sensei*, muttered an apology, and slipped past Erik. Spotting Nori, he hurried down the aisle and dropped into the empty seat. Erik ended up taking a chair in the back of the room next to Michiko.

The angels stopped singing.

Nori slumped forward onto her desk.

This day so totally sucked.

Evening shadows crept across the room by the time Nori finished up the last of her homework. As an incentive to get done quickly, she'd made a deal with herself that she wouldn't check her e-mails until she was through, but it had still taken her nearly two hours to do her assignment for culture class.

She flexed her aching fingers and rolled her neck to work

out the kinks. You'd think the Japanese could use just one set of characters for writing like everyone else, but no. They had to use four: *hiragana*, *katakana*, kanji, and *romanji*. Right now Nori was studying the phonetic characters. There were forty-six *hiragana* characters for Japanese words and just as many *katakana* characters for foreign words—and she'd had to copy every one of them. She didn't even want to think about kanji! There were thousands of those characters. The other form of writing was *romanji*, which was the Romanized letters she was used to, so at least she didn't have to worry about that.

The computer whirred softly as it booted up. With a quick clacking of keys, Nori typed in her password and logged onto her e-mail account. She'd sent Val a play-by-play of the past couple of days and was eager to see the response. Val always knew how to make Nori feel better.

Valerie Wexner had been Nori's one true BFF since second grade when she pushed Scott Gardner off the slide for teasing Nori about her "squinty eyes." Nori, in turn, had pulled out a handful of Danielle Smoot's hair when she made fun of Valerie's glasses. From that year forward, as Val's mom would say, the two were joined at the hip.

They completed each other, like yin and yang. Nori, an only child, grew up with discriminating taste. Val, as the fourth of six, learned to grab what she could get. While Nori's mom and dad were second-generation Japanese Americans who felt the need to prove themselves by "getting ahead,"

Val's laid-back parents were more than satisfied with their middle-class status. Nori studied hard in school. Val studied fashion and boys. Nori provided the social conscience. Val provided the social contacts.

If anyone should understand how Nori felt right now, it should be Val. At least that's what Nori expected.

From: Valerivalera@email.com
To: Revengelobster@email.com
Subject: Get a grip, girl

Whatsup? Did I detect a hint of self-pity in your last note? Snap out of it! Do you know what I would give to be in your shoes? The farthest I've ever traveled was to Cleveland and I bet the gas station restroom was ten times worse than those squatter toilets you described. (Waaaay too much information there, BTW.)

You're just homesick. You know that, right? A little culture shock going on. It will get better, I promise.

Bummer about Herr Hottie. But you have all summer, girl-friend. It's not over just because some bimbo is making the moves on him in class. Besides, what about Bushido Boy? He sounds like a winner. Why not hang with him?

Meanwhile, quit with the whining and have fun. You do remember how to do that, right?

Repeat after me: "I am Nori Tanaka. I have lots of friends. I am cute and popular. I know how to have a good time. I will

never send Val another boohoo e-mail or I will be forever cut off."

((((Hugs))))

Val

Nori frowned and turned off her computer. So much for understanding.

Val was wrong. This wasn't homesickness, culture shock, or any of that garbage. And it wasn't just Michiko's ice treatment, either. Everywhere Nori turned she felt like an outsider. The gaijins treated her differently because they assumed she was Japanese and the Japanese treated her differently because they knew she was a gaijin.

Her eyes slid over to Amberly, who was bent over her desk, the little pink tip of her tongue poking out of the corner of her mouth as she concentrated on forming kanji strokes with her bamboo brush. How fair was it that Airhead Amberly seemed so content when she, Nori, was miserable?

Amberly glanced up from her work.

"Uh...It looks good," Nori said quickly, hoping that what she'd been thinking didn't show on her face.

Amberly smiled her little Barbie-doll smile. "Thanks. It's for my project. I'm not any good at public speaking, so this is how I'm going to present my message."

"I see," Nori said, even though she didn't.

Someone knocked on the door.

"I'll get it!" Amberly jumped up and sashayed across the room, fluffing her hair as she went. Nori gritted her teeth and flipped open her history syllabus.

Atsushi stood at the door. Of course. Who else? "A group of us are going to Shibuya," he said. "You two want to come?"

Amberly leaned against the door frame, twisting her hair around her finger. "What are you going to do?"

Who cares? Nori was just so happy to be getting out of the room she could have kissed Atsushi, even if he was just inviting her out of duty.

"We're going to hang out, get something to eat."

Amberly had to rinse out her bamboo brushes before she could go, so Nori went down with Atsushi to wait for the rest of the group in the lobby.

"How do you like your classes so far?" he asked.

Well, there's a scintillating conversation starter. "They're okay," she said.

"Which one do you like best?"

Oh, brilliant. He's taking lessons from my mother. "You know what? I'd rather not talk about school."

"That bad?"

She shrugged. "I'll live."

"That's encouraging."

"It's the best I can do."

He sat on the low couch and patted the cushion beside

him. When she was settled, he leaned back, steepled his fingers, and raised an eyebrow at her. Just one eyebrow. It was kinda cute. "So tell me about these problems you're having. How do they make you feel?"

Despite herself, Nori laughed at his psychiatrist impersonation. She pulled her feet up so that she was sitting cross-legged and fingered the stitching on her shoe. "Well, Doctor, I don't know. Just...I keep making stupid mistakes with the language and everything. Doing the wrong things at all the wrong times. You know, stuff like that. Makes me feel like an idiot. Especially when certain people take such pleasure in correcting me."

He nodded sympathetically. "*Gambatte, ne?* It'll get better."

"Gam what?"

"*Gambatte.* It means hang in there. Deal with it."

"In other words, suck it up."

"Well, yeah."

Oh, sure. No one ever tells Amberly to *gambatte*. She makes worse mistakes, and everyone just thinks she's cute.

"G'day!" Kiah, in Reeboks and running shorts, strode across the lobby, her gray T-shirt dark with sweat.

"Back atcha," Atsushi said. "How was the run?"

"Long." She pushed her damp hair back from her beet red face and dropped onto the couch next to Nori.

"You went running in this heat?" Nori was impressed. Impressed that Kiah was insane.

"It's what I do. I'm on the cross-country team back home." She leaned her elbows on her knees, hands dangling. "So. What are we talking about?"

"Nothing."

"Actually," Atsushi said, drawing out the word, "Nori was just telling me how irresistible I am."

Nori laughed. "Yeah, you keep dreaming."

The laughter stopped abruptly when Michiko stepped up beside them, flanked by three other girls. She bowed in greeting and starting yammering away in Japanese. One of the sentences ended with a *"Ne?"* and Nori realized Michiko was directing the question at her.

"I'm sorry? What did you say?"

"Oh, *gomen nasai.* I am sorry. I forget that you do not speak Japanese." She batted her eyes innocently.

"So how 'bout you translate," Kiah retorted. "'Cause I don't do Japanese, either."

Michiko bowed again. "I do not wish for Nori to be embarrassed. I simply remind her that in Japan it is impolite to place one's shoes upon the furniture. The dirt—"

"Yeah, yeah. We get it." Kiah waved her off.

Nori shot Atsushi a look. See?

He raised his eyebrows, his look telling her to *gambatte.* Suddenly, going out didn't look like such an appealing alternative to sitting alone in the room. Not with Michiko in the mix.

Amberly finally arrived, out of breath, pink skin daintily flushed. She greeted everyone and said, "I'm sorry I took so long. I just about forgot my camera…"

Nori rolled her eyes. Oh, right. The camera. And how about that new outfit you're wearing and the extra coat of mascara?

"So, you going to come with us?" Atsushi asked Kiah.

"Sure. Give me ten." She hurried off to shower.

Nori grew quiet as Michiko dominated the conversation. Even Amberly, who was always the center of attention, withdrew a little.

Kiah returned, wet hair slicked back and tucked behind her ears. The group started to leave, but Nori hesitated. Michiko took her place beside Atsushi. When he reached the door, Atsushi looked back to Nori.

"You coming?"

"Oh, I, um…" She shook her head. "I better not. I just remembered an assignment I forgot to do. You go on."

"No. You've got to come."

Michiko placed a hand on his arm. "We will miss the train if we do not hurry."

"Go," Nori said. "I'll come next time."

"I could stay—"

"Look," Nori snapped, "you do not have to babysit me, okay? Just go." With that, she stomped to the elevator.

As the doors were about to close, Kiah grabbed one of

them to hold it back. "What's this? You going to let some bush pig make you wimp out?"

"Oh, you mean Michiko? No, I don't care about her. I've got homework. Really."

Kiah let the doors close, but not before Nori read the disbelief in her eyes.

Back in the room, Nori fingered her books. Ironically, she really did need to study. Just not right now. She heard the voices down below and rushed to the balcony to watch the group walking down the street, laughing and talking. Nori's chest felt tight. Maybe she should go with them after all. But then, there was Michiko, giggling and plucking at Atsushi's arm. Forget it.

Well, journal, it looks like it's just you and me, but I have no idea what to write. Mom says I'm supposed to record my happy memories. As if.

Maybe things wouldn't be so bad if I could work up the nerve to talk to Erik. But he's always with someone—like stupid, two-faced Michiko. The irony is that Erik is probably her toughest competition for the scholarship. If what Kiah says is true, Michiko is only after him to gain some kind of advantage over him. Why are guys so stupid?

And speaking of stupid, why the heck is Atsushi

friends with a troll like Michiko? I wish I could figure him out. He's considerate, he's attentive, and he's totally easy on the eyes...but I'm pretty sure he's only hanging around because he feels duty-bound to take care of me, and I do not want to be anyone's obligation.

Nori closed her journal and tried without much success to study before crawling off to bed. At least when she was sleeping, she could still pretend the whole Japan thing was going just the way she'd hoped it would.

Chapter Four

In ecology, Nori discovered that she really should have been doing her homework the night before. She totally flunked the pop quiz on their reading assignment.

The rest of the day didn't fare much better, and by the time culture rolled around, Nori had all but mentally checked out.

She hardly even looked at her handout—except for when she was drawing pictures and doodling in the margins. They were having a guest speaker anyway—Kikuchi-*san*, the diminutive school secretary who, as it turned out, also happened to be an expert on the history and art of Japanese

kimono. But she was talking so softly that Nori couldn't possibly understand her—even if she'd had the inclination to pay attention.

Wada-*sensei* strolled up and down the aisles during Kikuchi-*san*'s presentation. As he neared, Nori quickly slid the paper inside her notebook and tried to look as attentive as she could. Wada-*sensei* paused by her desk.

"Miss Tanaka."

She looked up innocently. "Yes?"

"You seem to be about the right size. Would you mind modeling for us?"

"I'm sorry?"

"The kimono."

"Oh. I don't think—"

"Go on." Atsushi prodded her from behind.

With a sigh, she stood and followed Wada-*sensei* to the front of the room, where Kikuchi-*san* stood holding a white robe-looking thing in her hands.

"This goes under the kimono," she said, handing it to Nori. "Please, you change in the girls' room and come back quickly."

Nori eyed the flimsy cotton thing, leaned close to Kikuchi-*san,* and said in a low voice, "You mean you want me to… uh…"

"That is right, Nori-*san*, change out of street clothes." Kikuchi-*san* smiled serenely and handed Nori some white socks and a pair of sandals. "Also please the *tabi* and *geta*.

They are difficult to put on once the kimono is in place. Quickly please. Class time is short."

Cussing under her breath, Nori took the robe and footwear and stomped down the hall to the girls' bathroom. Sure, why not? This was about the way her week was going. As if she didn't feel like a freak already, why not dress up like a doll in front of the whole class?

Inside a stall, she kicked off her shoes and pulled on the *tabi* socks. They looked like little foot mittens with a separate opening for the big toe. The sandals were just like flip-flops only the sole was made of stiff, black vinyl and the thong part of red padded fabric.

She hung up her clothes and wrapped the thin robe tightly around her waist, feeling totally naked. As she walked back to class, her *tabi* slipped against the smooth vinyl of the *geta* with each step so that she had to shuffle to keep the sandals on her feet. This was so *not* cool.

She paused at the doorway. Okay. Deep breath. She turned the handle, pushed open the door, and shuffled into the classroom.

Kikuchi-*san*'s gasp was as delicate as her features, but it stopped Nori cold. She looked down, half expecting to find the robe gaping open. "What?"

"Please, I am sorry, Nori-*san*." Kikuchi-*san* motioned for her to come forward. She took Nori by the shoulders and turned her back to the class, deftly untying the robe's sash. "Always wrap the right side over the body first, overlap with

left. Right on top of left is only to dress corpses for burial." She retied the robe properly.

Nori tried to ignore the sniggers as she turned around to face the class. Tried to ignore the burning in her cheeks. Could this be any more humiliating?

Absolutely.

"Notice that the kimono is cut straight," Kikuchi-*san* explained as she tied padding around Nori's waist. "We must fill out Nori-*san*'s body curves so the kimono will hang correctly."

Michiko whispered loudly, "What curves?" and was rewarded with a ripple of laughter.

Oh, just kill me now.

Kikuchi-*san* slipped a second robe on top of the padding, talking as she smoothed the fabric. "This robe is called *naga-juban*," she explained. "It gives collar definition to the kimono."

From the reading she had actually done, Nori knew the kimono had originally been worn in many colorful layers. In fact, noble ladies might have donned as many as thirty layers at a time. Such practice was not common anymore, but this kimono itself was pretty substantial. Intricately embroidered with long, flowing sleeves, the kimono's heavy silk background was a wash of deep sapphire near the hem, fading to sky blue above the waist. Flowers, bamboo, and tall white birds decorated the sleeves and skirt.

Kikuchi-*san* handled the kimono reverently as she helped Nori put it on. "Textiles such as the kimono have been very important to the Japanese since ancient times," she said. "It is said that when the angry sun goddess hid in a cave, bringing darkness to the world, other divinities enticed her out with a dance of blue and white textile banners."

She wrapped the kimono around Nori and tied it with a long string. "Please notice the pattern in this kimono. Bamboo and plum blossoms signify good luck and prosperity. The crane is a symbol of long life."

She lifted Nori's arms to demonstrate the length of the sleeves, which hung well past her waist. "Young, unmarried women wear long sleeves. These are called *furisode*. They can be sometimes as long as the ankles. You will notice the young women's colors are very vibrant, much like Nori-*san.*"

Again with the snickering. Nori wanted to crawl into the nearest hole.

Next came the elaborately woven obi sash. Kikuchi-*san* wrapped it twice around Nori's waist before tying it securely in the back.

"How one ties the obi has significance," she explained. "Married women wear a simple box bow, but Nori-*san* will wear the butterfly bow to show she is still available."

No sniggering this time. Try all-out laughter. Nori's blush burned all the way to the tips of her ears.

Unfazed, Kikuchi-*san* finished tying the bow and secured

the obi with a decorative silken rope. She stepped out from behind Nori and bowed deeply to the class. "Here you see the completed kimono," she said. "Questions?"

Michiko raised her hand. "Can you ask her to turn around?" she asked. "We'd like a better look at her big... bow."

The class erupted in laughter.

Michiko shot Nori a triumphant look. Nori narrowed her eyes. *Think I'm going to slink away again like last night? I don't think so.*

Pasting a smile on her face, she struck an exaggerated fashion model pose. In the kimono's narrow skirt, she walked a few mincing steps, pivoted, and posed again, glancing saucily over her shoulder.

The class laughed again, but this time with her, not at her. *Oh, yeah. The old Nori was back.*

She took her final bow just as the bell rang.

Michiko did not look pleased. Especially when Erik, whom she had obviously been trying to impress, turned away from her to load up his backpack.

"Nice show, Seaweed." Nori tore her eyes from Erik. Atsushi stood grinning before her.

"Not funny," she said.

"That's what you get for skipping out on us last night."

"I had to study."

"Yeah, yeah. Next time I'm not going to take—"

He broke off as Michiko sidled up to him and said something in Japanese. His response made her smile.

Nori bristled. "Well, I should get changed," she said. "See you later."

Atsushi left with Michiko. The rest of the class filed out while Nori waited impatiently for Kikuchi-*san* to unwind the obi and set her free. A couple of clueless girls paused to finger the kimono fabric and admire the obi's butterfly bow, ogling and yammering as if Nori was a store mannequin or something. One of them even lifted the hem of the kimono to look at the fabric of the *juban*.

Hello? Person standing here. Nori turned away.

And bumped directly into Erik Sussmann.

He grabbed her arm to steady her. "*Gomen nasai*," he apologized, the Japanese clipped in his strong German accent. She looked from the hand on her arm, tan and muscular and dusted with fine blond hair, to the broad-cheeked face, with eyes piercingly blue and fringed with golden lashes.

"Uh…"

He flashed a smile, showing off teeth so white and even, his orthodontist should be proud. "You are okay?"

"Yeah," she breathed.

His smile broadened, and he bowed. Only not the humble Japanese kind of bowing. No, he looked more like some Prussian prince. Some very hot Prussian prince. "I am Erik," he said. As if he had to tell her who he was.

Everything Nori had imagined she would say to him totally evaporated. All she could think to do was to bow in return.

Wada-*sensei*, who had been watching the exchange with irritatingly transparent amusement, said, "Allow me to make the introductions. Nori, this is Erik Sussmann from Germany. Erik, this is Nori Tanaka, one of our lovely Japanese students."

Nori opened her mouth to correct him, but Erik said, "Yes, I've noticed her around." His eyes never left hers.

Her stomach did a funny flippy thing. *He'd noticed her?* She fought the silly grin she knew was threatening to spread across her face. "I am pleased to meet you," she managed to say. Now that was an understatement.

"And I, you." He was looking at her with such intensity she thought she was going to melt. "Perhaps we could get together sometime? I would like to hear the Japanese perspective on many things."

"Oh. I . . . I'm not . . ."

He cocked his head to the side, looking her up and down. "You look very nice in the kimono," he said. "It suits you."

"You think so?"

"Yes. With your hair up you would look just like a geisha."

Uh, okay. And that would be a good thing, right? "Thank you," she said. I think.

Of course that was the moment Kikuchi-*san* decided it was time to begin undressing her model.

"I should go," Erik said. "I will see you around?"
Nori smiled and nodded. You can count on it.

Revengelobster: So then he met me after school and asked if I wanted to hang out with him when we go 2 sumo practice on Saturday. Wants a native 2 show him around.

Valerivalera: Helloo? UR not native.

Revengelobster: He doesn't know that.

Valerivalera: U don't think he will kind of figure it out? Correct me if I'm wrong, but don't believe U speak Japanese.

Revengelobster: Actually am picking it up rather quickly.

Valerivalera: Missing the point.

Revengelobster: We R supposed 2 use English anyway. Language of diplomacy, U know. And it's not like he speaks Japanese. How's he going 2 know if I make a mistake? Will be fine.

Valerivalera: Wouldn't play this charade if I were U.

Revengelobster: Good thing U R not me.

Valerivalera: So what are U going 2 do? Make up stuff and hope he buys it?

Revengelobster: Atsushi's going 2 help. He's a big sumo fan.

Valerivalera: Get out. How could U ask him 2 do that? Can't believe U.

Revengelobster: What? He doesn't mind.

That wasn't completely true. Atsushi had been against the idea from the start. But Nori's skills of persuasion (or, more likely, his sense of duty) finally won out, and he agreed. But mind? Well, yeah. He probably did.

> **Valerivalera::** What happens if someone blows UR cover?
> **Revengelobster:** Who's gonna even know? It's not like we have all our classes together or anything. Besides, everyone already thinks I'm Japanese.
> **Valerivalera:** Still don't get it. Why not just tell him the truth?

She had considered that option... for about thirty seconds. But he thought she was Japanese and was clearly attracted by the idea. Plus, he wanted a native guide. How could she blow that opportunity?

> **Revengelobster:** Really am Japanese, U know. Even if I nevr lived here before. Not really a lie.
> **Valerivalera:** Right. U are so going 2 hell.

Chapter Five

Nori and Atsushi met in the common room at midnight to watch the recap of the latest sumo tournament on TV. He'd said it was the only way he could think of to teach her what she needed to know about sumo wrestling, but she had a sneaking suspicion he just wanted an excuse to watch the thing.

She leaned toward him and whispered in his ear, "When are they actually going to do something?"

"Shhh." Atsushi waved a distracted hand at her, eyes glued to the screen. "Watch. This is a good match."

She flopped back against the couch cushions, rolling her
eyes. Good? All she'd seen so far were two massively obese
men in diapers, grunting and stomping and slapping themselves as they made angry faces at each other. Like those
cheesy professional wrestlers, for Pete's sake. Only sumos
were not all that great in the bod department. Now if they
had all been built like The Rock, that might be something...

"Watch," Atsushi ordered.

The men squatted down, assuming what Nori could only
imagine was an attack position.

"I'll bet that's not pretty from behind," she whispered.

"Shhh."

"What are we watching for?"

"Shhh."

"Why is the referee dressed up like that?"

"Shhh."

"What's that stuff the sumo's throwing?"

"Salt."

"Why?"

"To purify the ring. Now shush!"

"Hmmph."

The men squared off once again. Raised their legs high
on one side and then another. Stomped. Threw salt. Slapped
themselves. Yelled. Glared. And...charged like two angry
bull elephants.

Instantly, Atsushi was on the edge of his seat, fist pump-
ing the air.

And then it was over.

No lie, it took only like fifteen seconds before one of the tubbies was butt-down in the clay with a confused look on his face while the other strutted around the ring, trying to look manly.

"You're kidding me. That's all there is to it?"

"All there is? What are you saying? Sumo wrestling is an art as much as a sport. Hours of practice and sacrifice went into what you just saw."

"Uh-huh. So would you care to explain what it was I just saw? 'Cause I still don't get it."

Early the next morning, Nori stood waiting for the bus in the gray predawn light, rubbing the sleep out of her eyes and having second thoughts. This was crazy. It would never work. Until this point, she hadn't really thought through what fooling Erik would entail. Wouldn't he wonder why she didn't speak with a Japanese accent? What if he asked her to say something in Japanese or read kanji or something? And how was she supposed to behave? She was so dead.

She spied Michiko with several of her friends standing near the dorm entrance. Noticed how their posture was finishing-school perfect. How they clasped their hands demurely or fluttered them about in the air like butterflies as they talked. Nori straightened and tried her best to imitate the way Michiko daintily brushed her silky black hair away from her face with the back of her hand.

Atsushi stepped up beside Nori. "What are you doing?"

She half smiled and shrugged. "Just getting into character."

He snorted and shook his head. "You don't have to do this."

"I'll be fine," she said, as much to herself as to him.

"That's not what I mean," he muttered, but Nori didn't pay attention. She was too busy looking for Erik.

Entering the practice arena, Nori realized why they called the place a stable; it smelled like a herd of sweaty Holsteins lived there.

Wada-*sensei* showed the group where to sit. "This area is reserved for the stable master," he said, "and for honored guests to watch practice. Please remember to act like honored guests and be quiet. Oh, and remember to take off your shoes."

On the platform, Nori knelt as she saw the other Japanese girls doing, although she probably would have been much more comfortable sitting cross-legged like Erik and Atsushi, who sat beside her. While the two of them whispered animatedly—no doubt discussing the finer points of sumo—Nori took in the atmosphere of the stable.

The room was paneled in light-colored wood, with wooden slats near the packed-earth floor for ventilation and barred windows to let in the light. On one wall hung dozens of small wooden tags with kanji characters written on them.

In a clay circle in the middle of the room, the sumos

stretched, squatted, grunted, yelled, and slapped a wooden pole. Why they did the latter, Nori couldn't say, and she was not about to ask Atsushi in front of Erik.

At first she squirmed at the sight of all the blubber and buttocks in front of her. But as the practice wore on, she found herself admiring the skill and agility the sumos displayed and hardly noticed their state of undress at all.

Atsushi caught her eye as the matches began. "See, you like it, don't you?"

She shrugged. "It's way better in person than it was on TV. They're not doing all that posturing and ritual stuff here."

Wada-*sensei* signaled for them to be quiet, and they turned their attention back to the ring.

When practice was over, the students stood and bowed to the sumos while Wada-*sensei* expressed their deepest gratitude. At least that's what Nori assumed he was saying. He was speaking in rapid Japanese, but she caught a few key words along the way.

Outside the stable, he gathered the group together. "Listen up! You have the rest of the school day to explore Ryogo-ku. This is the sumo district, so there is a lot to see." He pulled a packet of papers from his bag. "Here are maps of the area. On these you can find where there are more stables and even a sumo museum in the stadium. Whatever you do, behave yourselves and meet back at the station at two thirty, understood?"

Atsushi turned to Nori and Erik. "Do you mind if I hang with you guys?" he asked smoothly.

"Sure," Nori answered, in case Erik was tempted to decline. "We don't mind, do we, Erik?"

He shrugged. "No, it is fine."

Before long, Atsushi and Erik were so deep in conversation that Nori was sure she could disappear and neither would even notice. Not that she had any intention of disappearing.

As much as she wasn't into the sumo thing, Nori did get a weird kind of thrill when they were walking down a side street and three big sumos in blue-and-white *yukata* lumbered toward them going the other way. She tried not to stare as they passed, but they were really a magnificent sight to behold. Their *yukata* robes looked like kimono, but were made of a thin, cotton material and didn't have any of the cumbersome underlayers. They wore wooden sandals, and their hair was oiled and pulled into ponytails high on their heads.

Erik lowered his voice. "Do they usually walk around in public dressed like that?"

"Of course," Atsushi said.

Well, better that than the diapers.

"So, Nori," Erik said, "where in Japan do you live?"

She tried to ignore Atsushi's raised brow when she said, "I'm staying in the dorms here, but I have family in Kyoto." Well, it was the truth, wasn't it? Not her immediate family, but still.

"Ah, Kyoto," said Erik. He draped his arm around her shoulder, and Nori's heart went all fluttery at his touch. "I have always wanted to visit," he said. "What is it like? Do the geisha really walk around the streets in their kimono?"

"Sometimes," she managed to say. She was pretty sure that was also true. "Um, are you getting hungry? Should we find someplace to eat?"

Atsushi showed them to a restaurant that was owned by a retired sumo champion where they served the same kind of *chanko nabe* stew that sumos eat.

"It's really good," he said. "You'll like it."

Was he crazy? It was much too hot to be eating stew. Still, Nori followed happily when Erik said he'd like to try it.

The entrance to the restaurant featured an elaborate swooped-roof facade and a row of sumo-themed banners lined up in front. But inside, the restaurant itself was rather small. On all the walls hung wooden plaques with kanji pronouncements, faded silk tournament aprons, and several aged, framed photographs of fierce-looking sumo.

The waiter sat them at a square table that had a small cookstove inset in the center. He turned on the burner and set a pot of water on top of it, then handed them tall, narrow menus. Written in kanji.

Erik scooted his chair closer to Nori's. "What does this say?" he asked, pointing to the inside of his menu.

She quickly glanced at Atsushi for help, but he remained silent, a smirk tugging at the corners of his lips. Clearly he

enjoyed her panic. "It's, um...it just lists the kinds of stews available." She sure hoped she was right. Shooting Atsushi a pointed look, she said, "What sounds good to you?"

"Everything." He stretched back in his chair. "Why don't you choose?"

Nori closed her menu and glared at him. "No. I think I'll leave it up to you. I'm not really all that hungry."

"What varieties are there?" Erik asked.

"Atsushi, could you tell him?" She stood up. "I need to visit the ladies' room."

She had no idea where the restrooms were located, but she escaped to the back of the restaurant anyway. Wandering down a narrow corridor, she passed a couple of doors that could have been bathrooms or linen closets or trash incinerators for all she knew; they were all labeled in kanji. Fine. She'd just stand here for a while until—

"Nori-*san*?" Wada-*sensei* exited one of the doors, wiping his hands with a handkerchief.

"Yeah. Hi," she said with a weak smile. "I was just going back to sit down."

"You're eating here?"

Well, duh. "Um, yeah. I'm here with Atsushi and Erik."

He followed her back to the table. "That's what I like to see—experiencing the culture," he said, nodding to Erik.

Nori took her seat next to Erik. "Saw him in the back," she explained.

"Are you alone?" Atsushi asked Wada-*sensei*. "Would you care to join us?"

Nori kicked him under the table. He gave her a look that said, What?, and pulled out the chair for Wada-*sensei* to sit. She had no choice but to welcome her teacher and hope he wouldn't say anything to blow her cover.

"Thank you. That's very nice of you." Wada-*sensei* sat. "Have you decided what to order?"

They settled on the pork and beef. Soon, the waiter returned to their table carrying a tray laden with meat, vegetables, tofu, and some pale *udon* noodles. He warmed ladles of paste before stirring them into the water with long chopsticks.

"That's miso," Atsushi said to Erik. "The red is salty and brings out the sweetness of the white."

When the broth was ready, the waiter began adding ingredients with his chopsticks, emptying the tray. He stirred the pot, adjusted the heat, bowed, and then he was gone.

Wada-*sensei* rubbed his hands together, breathing in the savory scent. "Isn't this great? I love this stuff."

Nori had to admit the stew was very good. It was just much too hot to eat on such a sweltering day. She picked at her food while the guys wolfed theirs down. Sated and lazy, they sat around the table for a while longer, talking.

"I've lived in Japan for ten years now," Wada-*sensei* said in response to a question from Erik.

Nori sat up straight. "You're not from here?"

"Naw. I'm from California. Bay area. But my wife's from Chofu. We met at UC Berkeley."

"Did you speak Japanese before you moved here?"

"Sure. My parents were real big into the whole ancestral heritage thing. Besides regular American school, I had to go to Japanese school every Saturday. Really messed up my sports schedule."

Nori's parents had never suggested she go to Japanese school. They never talked about her ancestry or anything like that; they were always too busy trying to make sure she was American enough to fit in despite her Asian looks. She realized sadly that instead of being proud of her Japanese heritage like Wada-*sensei* was, she had grown up defensive, afraid to be labeled as "different."

"...and so I took the teaching job here at the International School, and I've never looked back."

"What was it like?" Nori blurted. "Coming here, I mean. Did you like it right away?"

"Oh, sure," Wada-*sensei* replied. "It was like finding a piece of my life that had been missing. But it wasn't always easy." He leaned forward, cradling his teacup in both hands, and looked Nori in the eye. "You know how it is. When you come over here looking like this, people expect you to know a whole lot more than you can learn in Japanese school. I wasn't afforded the same patience a regular gaijin might get. At first, it was quite hard; the one place I thought I would really fit in, I didn't. Not for a long time." He took a sip of his green tea and smiled wryly. "They're used to me now, of course."

Nori shifted in her seat. That was too close. Ironic, wasn't it? Now that she had found someone who might understand what she was feeling, she couldn't talk to him about it.

The grossest thing I learned today: Sumos never wash their little diaper things. (Called, ironically, mewashi. Should have been called nobodywashi. ☺) How nasty is that? They believe if they wash the mewashi, all the sumo's experience will be washed away as well.

The coolest thing: Erik is a Libra, like me. Not that I'm into that kind of stuff, but he said it made us compatible, so who am I to argue?

The most painful thing I learned today: my sandals are so not walking shoes. By the time we reached the Nihonbashi Bridge, I had huge blisters the size of dimes where the straps kept rubbing. The upside is that Atsushi and Erik took turns giving me piggyback rides back to the train. Every cloud and all that...

Chapter Six

By Tuesday, Nori was beginning to wonder if the whole pig-gyback thing had been such a good idea after all. Had it turned Erik off? He deigned to nod at her in class and answer with a casual "*konnichiwa*" when she said hi, but other than that, he wasn't going out of his way to be friendly.

Maybe he found out that she was scamming him. Or maybe he just plain wasn't interested. She didn't even want to consider that.

Val was no help.

• • •

TO: revengelobster@email.com
FROM: valerivalera@email.com
SUBJECT: Re:Trouble in Paradise

Hey, girl.

Bummer. No fun getting caught in your tangled web, huh? Can I just say this serves you right for lying to HH in the first place? Not what you want to hear, I know, so here's what you do. If he won't come to you, go to him. You make the move. Shouldn't be too tough after the act you've been putting on. Just ask him to be partners on your next outing or something. Make sure he knows the ball is in his court. Oh, and then you should tell the guy the truth.

Good luck!

V

She was probably right. At least about the asking-him-out part. The truth could come later, once she knew he was interested. But…what if he wasn't? She would totally die.

Meanwhile, Michiko seemed to be everywhere Erik was, so even if Nori had had the guts to approach him, she'd never get the chance to talk to him alone. Not without raising Michiko's antenna. She'd find out what Nori was up to and when she did, you can bet she'd be more than happy to out her to Erik.

Nori was tempted to tell Erik what Kiah said about

Michiko's scholarship strategy, but that would only make her look petty and jealous. All she could do was hope Erik was smart enough not to fall into Michiko's trap.

Atsushi caught up with Nori as she walked to the train station after school. "What's with the face?"

"Born with it."

"So. It is worse than I thought." He stroked his chin and raised one brow. "This is going to take serious intervention. What do you have going on tonight?"

"Absolutely nothing," she said. Wasn't that the sad truth.

"Ah. No pressing homework or projects?"

"Not really. Why?"

"We should get out, go do something."

She glared at him. "You do not have to entertain me."

"Whoa." He took a step back, raising his hands. "Where did that come from? Look, it's me, okay? I need to get out. And you're going to come with me."

"No, I—"

"Nuh-uh. You blew me off last time. You're coming."

Four hours later, Nori found herself pressed up against Atsushi on a crowded train bound for Shibuya. Not an altogether unpleasant experience, she realized with some reluctance. No. Don't go there. At some point he's going to wake up and decide you're no longer his responsibility.

The train rounded a corner, and the passengers swayed

in unison. Nori struggled to keep her balance, and Atsushi slipped his arm around her waist to hold her up.

"Do you ever get used to this?" she asked.

He waggled his eyebrows. "Not yet, but I could."

She would have slugged him if she could have just moved her hand. "I mean the crowds."

"Nothing to get used to," he said with a shrug. "It's what I grew up with."

"Well, it almost makes me miss Ohio."

"Ah. So you are a small-town girl at heart."

"I said *almost.*"

"Hey, I'm not knocking it. I liked it when I lived there. But I like the lights of the city, too."

The train pulled into Shibuya station.

"Hold on," Atsushi said, taking her hand. "It's going to get a little crazy."

"A little crazy" was the understatement of the year. Shibuya station was complete pandemonium. People rushing back and forth. Too many tides to fight. And the noise! "Just wait," Atsushi shouted. "You ain't seen nothing yet."

They fought their way through a station door that led out to an open square. Well, open was relative. Hordes of people swarmed around them as Nori stopped to gape at the lights. It reminded her of the time she visited Times Square, only magnified. Flashing lights, illuminated billboards, and neon covered the tall buildings surrounding the square.

Several even had huge LED screens on the sides of them that had to be at least four stories high. Musicians and street hawkers competed with the TVs for an audience, adding to a confusion of noise that came from nowhere and everywhere at once.

"Wow" was all she could say. She felt like the country mouse getting her first glimpse of the big city.

Nori spotted a Japanese Goth couple strutting across the square, complete with matching six-inch platform boots, eighties punk-rock hairdos, and black lipstick. She giggled and tried not to stare.

They weren't the only spectacle. There were also leather-clad gangbanger look-alikes, schoolgirls in their plaid skirts and white leg warmers (in the summer!), businessmen (or salarymen, as Atsushi called them) all buttoned up in suits and ties, tackily dressed tourists, and about every other imaginable walk of life.

A gaggle of platinum-haired girls strolled by in matching ultrashort baby-doll dresses, platform Mary Janes, and white socks that came past up their knees. Each one of them was toting some sort of oversized baby toy—a stuffed animal or a pacifier.

"Bizarre," Nori said.

Atsushi smiled. "See, this is why I love Shibuya. Now check out this intersection over here." He took her shoulders and turned her so that she was facing toward the middle of the buildings. "Watch when the light changes."

It was one of the wildest things she'd ever seen. Well, okay, she was from Smallsville, Ohio, so she hadn't actually seen too many wild things, but this was way up there. When the pedestrian light turned green, hundreds of people swarmed out into the intersection. Not in crosswalks or anything like that, but all over the road like an army of ants.

"It's called a scramble intersection," Atsushi shouted over the noise.

"I can see why."

"Supposed to be the busiest intersection in the world."

No doubt.

"And this," he said, directing her attention back to the square, "is the most famous landmark gathering place in Shinjuku." He pointed to a statue on a pedestal in front of the station.

"A dog?"

"That's *Hachiko*," he said incredulously, as if the name should have some significance to her. "You know, as in Hachiko Square."

"They named this place after a dog?"

"Well, yeah." He cleared his throat and said in a tour-guide voice, "Hachiko, the loyal dog who continued to come to the station every day for ten years, looking for his master, who had died. When Hachiko passed away, this statue was erected in his honor in the very spot the dog had faithfully waited."

"Aw, that's sad."

"It's supposed to be inspiring. We Japanese are very big on loyalty, you know." He glanced at his watch. "Come on. If we hurry—"

"Oh, wait." Nori caught a flash of jewelry from one of the vendors' carts. "I want to look at those."

He frowned, but followed her to the cart.

Most of the jewelry was cheap and gaudy, but she liked the simplicity of some jade pendants hanging from black silk cords. They were carved in various shapes, with kanji characters inset in gold.

"What do they say?"

Atsushi translated. They were straightforward: peace, serenity, prosperity. Nori chose one that meant luck. She started digging through her purse, but Atsushi said, "I got it."

"Oh. No. You don't have to—"

"Don't worry about it. It's less than a thousand yen. Ten bucks. Like it's really going to break me." He paid the vendor, who put the pendant into a little silk pouch. Atsushi handed the pouch to Nori. "There. Now let's go." He took her hand and pulled her with him. "There's something I want to show you."

When she was younger, Nori's dad had taken her on a trip to Chicago. They ate deep-dish pizza and Chicago-style hot dogs, went boating on the lake and to a Cubs game, and looked out over the city from the top of the Sears Tower. The

Tokyo Metropolitan Government Building, where she and Atsushi were now, totally had Sears beat.

It wasn't the height; Nori doubted it was any taller. It was the view. From the observation deck, you could see the lights of Tokyo stretch on forever—or so it seemed.

"If you come up here in the daytime you can see Fuji," Atsushi said, "but this is the best view, I think."

She nodded solemnly.

"Hey, this is supposed to be fun. What's wrong?"

"Just thinking," Nori murmured. "My dad would love this."

The next day, under the acacia tree in the school courtyard, Nori shredded her paper napkin. Her Diet Coke had long since gone warm. Where was Atsushi? They hadn't made plans or anything, but he had shown up for lunch every day this term, and she was sort of counting on it. She wanted to tell him again what a great time she'd had last night.

They had barely made it back in time for curfew, which would totally have sent her mom over the edge. On a school night! And she was up even later finishing her homework after they got home. But it was so worth it.

They had talked and laughed up on the observation deck until the guard came and kicked them out at closing time. On the way home, they stopped at a café for a soda. Conversation came fast and easy, and before they knew it, it was past eleven.

It seemed like a perfect evening. So why didn't he come for lunch? Had she done something wrong? What was it with her and guys, anyway? They go out, she thinks they have a great time, but afterward the guy totally avoids her. First Erik and now Atsushi. It was enough to give a girl a complex.

Nori gathered her things to head inside where it was air-conditioned when she spotted Atsushi near the kiosk. With Michiko. Jeez, that girl was everywhere. Nori crumpled her paper bag. So what? Big deal. Atsushi and Nori were friends, that's all. He didn't owe her anything.

Chapter Seven

Nori walked into culture class to find Erik was already there. Alone. He looked up from the book he was reading, a grin spreading across his face when he saw her.

"*Konnichiwa*," she said.

"Nori!" His face shone with such genuine pleasure that Nori wondered why she'd been worried. "How are you?"

"Good. And you? I haven't seen you around much."

He shrugged. "Homework. You know."

They talked until the first bell rang. She was perfectly content and didn't feel the need to pursue it further.

But then Atsushi walked in with Michiko, and something

just snapped inside her head. She didn't even have time to think about what she was saying when she turned to Erik and blurted, "You doing anything tonight? A bunch of us are going to...uh...go to a karaoke place. Should be fun."

"Yes," he said. "I would like that."

About that time, Wada-*sensei* entered the room, and class began. Erik took his cue and strolled to the back of the room. He took his seat next to Michiko.

The latter looked up and caught Nori's eye, giving her a smug smile that, on a normal day, Nori would have felt compelled to remove from her face. At the moment, however, she didn't have time to think about that. Her mind was still churning from what she'd just done. How could she have asked Erik out? And to karaoke! She didn't know any karaoke places. And what if she couldn't get "a group of us" to go with them? She would look totally stupid.

Atsushi slipped into his seat and tapped her on the shoulder. "Hi," he whispered.

"Hi, yourself."

"Did you get your homework done last night?"

"Yeah. You?"

"Barely."

Nori twisted in her chair to face him, somehow managing to blink innocently when she said, "Hey, Atsushi, I was thinking. We should get a group together and go do something tonight. Like karaoke. Is there someplace close we could go?"

She ignored the little pang of guilt she felt when his face lit up. "Sure. I know the perfect place," he said.

Now all she had to do was get a group together.

After school, she discovered one of the distinct advantages of having a social butterfly for a roommate. All Nori had to do was say the word, and Amberly did the rest. By dinner, Amberly had invited Kiah and her roommate, Kirsti, Teruo and Yoshi, and a couple of others Nori didn't know. They all met outside the dorms around eight.

"We can walk from here," Atsushi told them. "It's right down the street."

Nori and Erik strolled a few paces behind the rest of the group so that they could talk. She was careful to steer the conversation away from herself.

"Tell me about your home," she said.

"I live in Stuttgart," Erik said. "You would like it. Lots of clubs and cafés. We even have a castle or two. Perhaps you can visit someday."

Oh, yes. This was turning out quite well. Nori looked up at him from under her lashes. "Perhaps."

The karaoke club was like nothing Nori had ever seen before. Instead of one stage in a bar or something, it was divided into dozens of private rooms. Theirs was about the size of a large closet. They filed into the room, taking seats around the U-shaped couch. The microphones lay on the

center table, with the karaoke machine mounted on the wall. Atsushi turned it on, and a mirrored disco ball over their heads started up as well, sending little squares of light dancing through the room.

Nori sat between Atsushi and Erik, thumbing through the book of songs in which both American and Japanese singles were listed. Nori slid a glance at Erik, hoping he wouldn't ask her to sing any of the Japanese ones.

Amberly was the first to take the stage. Of course. But you could have knocked Nori over with a chopstick when her selection came up. Perfect little Amberly singing AC/DC? No way. And yet there she was, belting out "Dirty Deeds Done Dirt Cheap."

"My dad was a rocker," she explained when she sat down. She straightened her skirt demurely. "Hard-core."

That broke the ice, and for the rest of the hour they sang nonstop. And, as is the way with karaoke, old Elvis and Beatles tunes kept popping up.

In fact, when it was almost time to leave, Erik grabbed the mike. He swiveled his hips and said in a truly horrible Elvis impersonation, "Thank you, thank you very much." Please. Guttural German accent and Elvis? Not a good combination.

But when he sang? Oh, mama. His rich, deep baritone voice sent shivers right through her. Oh, yes. Brawn, brains, *and* talent. Who could ask for more?

•　•　•

FROM: rtanaka@email.com

TO: revengelobster@email.com

SUBJECT: Miss You

Hi, Muffin.

How are you enjoying Japan? Hope you are having a good time. Haven't heard from you, but suppose I can consider no news as good news, yes? Still, a letter each week, as agreed, would be greatly appreciated.

Has gotten rather lonely around the house with you gone, but it's worth it to me just thinking about all the adventures you must be having. Your father stays at his apartment most nights.

How is your conference presentation shaping up? Study hard, Sweetie. Make me proud.

With love,

Mom

Nori stared at the screen. The high she'd been on since the karaoke party that night completely evaporated. "Your father stays at his apartment," it said. So he'd moved out? Love how Mom dished that little tidbit of information.

The walls of the tiny room started closing in on her. She couldn't breathe. Pushing away from her desk, she rushed out to the balcony, but the muggy air outside was just as stale and suffocating. So this was it? It was really happening.

"You okay?" Amberly stood hesitantly by the sliding door.

Nori took a deep breath and swiped the back of her hand over her eyes before turning around. "Yeah, just…" She couldn't think of anything to say. Just what? Spinning out of control?

Amberly nodded, not needing to hear the words. She faded back into the room. Nori stood on the balcony for a little while longer. When she went back inside, Amberly was lying on her futon. Nori could tell by the uneven breathing and stiff pose that Amberly was pretending to sleep. A little obvious, but Nori appreciated the space to sort through her feelings.

She wandered back over to her desk and sat in front of the computer. Taking a deep breath, she read through the e-mail one more time and then hit the reply button. If her mom could gloss over the bad news, Nori could, too.

FROM: revengelobster@email.com
TO: rtanaka@email.com
SUBJECT: Re: Miss you

Hello, Mom.

Thanks for your note. Yes, I am having a good time and studying hard. I was planning on writing Saturday, on P-day. That's what they call preparation day—our only day off. We have class every other day except Sunday, but that's when we go around and see the sights. They keep us very busy.

So, when did Daddy get an apartment? Where is it?

I should get back to my homework. I'll write more on Saturday.

Hugs to you,

Nori

She pressed send, wondering just what she was supposed to be feeling right now. Sadness? Anger? Hopefully nothing, 'cause she just wanted to be numb. This thing had been coming for a long time; they all knew it. But the timing! Sure. Wait until the kid is too far away to do anything about it. Was that supposed to make it hurt less? Not working. It just made her feel helpless. Only thing she could do from this distance was to put it out of her mind.

Anyway, thinking about Erik was much more fun. Tonight he'd asked her if she would show him around Akihabara. Panicked, she had cornered Atsushi on the way home to ask for help.

"Just one more time?" she begged.

For what seemed like a very long time, he didn't answer her. She was beginning to think that maybe he hadn't heard her and was about to ask again when she caught the look in his eye. Oh, yeah. He'd heard her all right. And he wasn't happy about it.

"Do you have any idea how insane this is?"

"I know it is. It's just…I can't explain it right now."

Atsushi folded his arms across his chest. "Well, you're going to have to if you want my help."

She dropped her gaze. "Okay. It's like this. Erik wants someone local to show him around. If he thinks I am that someone, it will give him the chance to get to know me better, and then he won't care if I'm Japanese or not."

Atsushi snorted. "If you really believe that, you're a whole lot dumber than you look."

"Hey!"

"This is not a good idea, Nori."

"Please. Just this once."

"Forget it." He shook his head, looking at her like she was an errant child. "Why would you want to go out with someone who doesn't like you for who you are? There are people you don't have to lie to, Nori."

"I'll tell him."

"What?"

"You come with us to Akihabara, and I promise I'll come clean. I just need some time to figure out how to do it."

When he finally relented, Nori should have felt relief, but she didn't.

Everything just seemed out of focus. Erik, Atsushi, her mom, her dad. It was way too much for one night.

On the train to Akihabara, Nori and Erik "accidentally" ran into Amberly and Atsushi, who casually suggested they hang out together.

Inviting Amberly along was a risk, since she had no idea what Nori was doing with Erik, but it was a risk Nori had to take. She didn't know her way around Akihabara, so she needed Atsushi, but she was afraid that Erik might be put off if they went out as a threesome again. Besides, Nori was pretty sure Amberly would be sufficiently distracted that she wouldn't say anything to give her away.

The train ride started off well enough. All they talked about were classes and classmates, teachers and projects. She began to relax a little, until Amberly said, "What's so exciting about Akihabara, anyway?"

Erik looked at Nori expectantly. She cleared her throat, but Atsushi didn't seem to get the hint. "Well," she began, tentatively trying to remember what she'd read online that afternoon, "it's only the largest electronics district in the world. They sell everything from digital watches to home appliances. You have to see it to believe it."

"Oh?" Amberly looked surprised. "You've been here before?"

"Uh…"

Out the window, Nori could see them approaching a section of town lit with enough neon and bright signs to rival Las Vegas. She blinked, trying not to let her wonder show since this was something she was supposed to have seen many times before.

"Look," she said. "Here we are." Like no one else could see the train was stopping.

Atsushi took the lead in the station, guiding them to the correct exit to reach the main drag of Akihabara Electric Town. "So," he said, "what's everyone looking for?"

Erik eyed the brightly lit stores along Chuo Street like a little kid on Christmas morning. "Computer games, laptops, anime, everything!"

"Well, we can start at Laox if you just want to check out the new stuff, but if you want to buy, we go to the backstreets. You'll get a better deal."

"Much better," Nori agreed.

Amberly knit her brows. "I'd like to look at cameras." She looked right at Nori. "Where do you suggest I go?"

"Oh, uh…" Nori's eyes darted about, searching for a store name not written in kanji. "There are so many camera stores here, and they're all about the same. Why don't we just walk around and see what interests you?"

The answer seemed good enough—for the moment. They strolled from store to store, fighting the crowds, laughing at the techno geeks, and marveling at the latest in cell phones, cameras, computers, plasma TVs, about anything electronic you could imagine. Digitized music and electronic beeps and chimes mingled with the rush of traffic on the street like white noise.

Amberly found the cameras and soon lost interest in anything else but examining tiny digital models no larger than a credit card. "Can you believe this?" she breathed. "Look at the resolution!"

They played with the latest Game Boys and zoomeroid ro-
bots, danced to an impromptu jazz session at an electronic
instruments store, and walked up and down streets until
Nori's feet ached.

All night, Nori avoided looking at Atsushi. Whenever he
did manage to catch her eye, he'd raise his brows and jerk
his head toward Erik and mouth, "Tell him." She'd nod reas-
suringly. She would tell him. Just not yet.

In a cell phone store Erik picked up a model with a built-
in GPS and turned it over in his hands. "Look at this! A hand-
held navigation system. Isn't it strange how a country so
technologically advanced can be backward in so many
ways?"

Atsushi's eyes narrowed. "Such as?"

"Oh, you know," Erik said, waving a hand dismissively.
"Antiquated medical system, power lines are all above-
ground, women viewed as second-class citizens, that sort of
thing."

"I know what you mean," Nori agreed.

Atsushi turned abruptly. "We should be getting back," he
snapped.

Nori's heart dropped. "Oh, I'm sorry. I didn't mean—"

"You know, I think I'd like to get that camera," Amberly
said. "Nori, why don't you come with me, and we can meet
the guys at the station?"

Nori blanched. What was she supposed to say? If she
went with Amberly, she wasn't sure how to find her way

back. They had walked around so much that all the streets looked the same. She looked to Atsushi for help, but he simply folded his arms and returned her pleading stare with a stony one. His single raised brow, which Nori found to be rather charming in most instances, only annoyed her now. So he enjoyed watching her squirm? Fine. Be that way. "Sure, Amberly," she said coolly, "let's go."

As soon as they rounded the corner, Amberly grabbed Nori's arm. "Okay, spill it," she demanded. "What is going on?"

"What are you talking about?"

"You. Acting like... I don't know. Just... not yourself."

Nori forced a laugh. "Oh, that." She stalled, trying to come up with something quick. Amberly would never understand the whole lying thing. "I was just... practicing. You know, for culture class. We, um... we have to be a tour guide for somewhere in Tokyo, and I chose here, but I can see I really need to learn more about it before I turn in my report."

That made absolutely no sense whatsoever, but it seemed to pacify Amberly for the time being. "So what was that between you and Atsushi just now? Are you supposed to be practicing being rude?"

"We were just joking. He wanted to do Akihabara, too, but I got it first." Nori even managed a carefree shrug with that one. It was scary how easy this lying thing was becoming.

Confusion pinched Amberly's perfect features. "Oh," she said, and that was it.

For now.

Chapter Eight

P-days would have been a lot more fun if there hadn't been so much to do. Really. Who wants to spend all day buried under laundry and homework? Boooring.

Nori slipped into a pair of cutoff sweatpants and her dad's old Buckeyes T-shirt, pulled her hair into a haphazard ponytail, and hauled her dirty clothes down the hall to the laundry room. There were only two washing machines and one dryer for like twenty girls, so of course everything was full.

Kiah, sitting cross-legged on the floor with an open book on her lap, glanced up as Nori walked in. "G'day, Nori! How you been?"

"Good. And you?"

"Can't complain." She eyed Nori's laundry. "You might have a wait. I already called the next machine."

"No worries. I'll check the other floors."

She waved good-bye and set off in search of a free machine. She finally scored two on the third floor.

Japanese washing machines looked like little playhouse things—small and rounded with little bubble windows on the front. Not at all like the large-capacity model at home. Each one could hold maybe two pairs of pants and three shirts or vice versa. She loaded both machines and settled in with her homework for the duration.

It wasn't until she had finished her laundry and stood waiting for the elevator that she noticed a group of guys sitting in the common area, noisily playing cards. All this time she had been on the boys' floor! Normally that would be a welcome scenario, but at the moment she looked hideous. She tried to make herself invisible and prayed that the elevator would arrive before any of the guys noticed her.

"Nori!"

Too late.

She turned toward the voice, at once elated and mortified to find Erik jogging down the hall after her. Resisting the urge to smooth down her hair or lick her lips, she managed to meet his eye. "*Konnichiwa*, Erik-*san.*"

"I love when you say that," he said, with an achingly cute smile. "What are you doing here?"

"Laundry," she said simply, and followed his gaze down to the basket in her hands. Her stomach lurched. There, right on top, lay her padded bra, the molded cups rising proudly like twin hills from a valley of clothes. Shifting the basket quickly to her other hip, she forced a smile. Please tell me you didn't notice that. "So, um, how 'bout you? What are you doing?"

"Nothing at the moment." He propped an arm against the wall. "Would you like to go get something to eat?"

Nori's mind raced through the homework she had yet to finish. "Uh…" She could always do it later. "Sure. Just let me get changed. I'll meet you in the lobby in ten?"

He leaned close, his whisper tickling her ear. "I will be waiting," he said.

Nori's legs went weak. She almost didn't hear the elevator chime or notice the door slide open. It was all she could do to stumble aboard and press the correct button for her floor.

Amberly was kneeling at her desk, diligently working on her calligraphy, when Nori rushed into the room. She glanced up, eyebrows puckered. "What is it? Is everything all right?"

"Oh, yeah." Nori pushed her clean clothes into the closet and turned to face Amberly triumphantly. "Erik Sussmann just asked me out."

"Uh-huh." Amberly seemed unimpressed. "Didn't you just go out with him on Thursday?"

"Well, yeah, but we were just sightseeing then. This is different. Like a date."

"That wasn't a date?"

"Not really, no," Nori said peevishly. What was up with the attitude?

Amberly put down her brush. "I apologize. It's very exciting. Got it. So, where are you going?"

"I don't know. Somewhere to eat."

"Okay, more important—what are you going to wear?"

Nori's smile faded. "Um..." She had absolutely no idea. Most of what she packed was the same old navy, green, and white school regulation colors. How boring was that? There were some clothes that Val had insisted she pack, but without Val there to guide her, Nori had no idea what to pair with what. She didn't have an eye for that kind of thing.

Amberly pushed away from her desk. "Okay," she said, "let's see what you've got."

Nori opened the closet.

Amberly sorted through Nori's clothes, selecting, discarding, and finally borrowing a bit from her own wardrobe to put together an outfit. When she was through, Nori stood in front of the mirror and all she could say was "Oh."

She turned in a circle, boho skirt swishing about her legs. With her cotton blouse, Amberly's chunky beads, and a wide leather belt to accentuate her tiny waist, Nori was looking good, if she didn't say so herself.

"Thanks, Amberly," she said, fingering the beads.

"Hey, no problem. Want me to do your makeup?"

Nori shook her head and backed away. "Uh, no, thanks."

When she stepped onto the elevator, a strange combination of butterflies and knots tumbled around in her stomach. Maybe she should've let Amberly have at her with the Clinique. Maybe she should've worn her hair up instead of down. Maybe—

Ping!

The elevator door slid open, and Nori stepped out into the lobby. Erik's whistle of appreciation was all the reassurance she needed.

"Wow," he said.

"Wow, yourself." And wow was right, even though he was just in T-shirt and jeans. Jeans that were worn and molded in all the right places. Mercy. "So...what do you feel like?"

"Pardon?" He grinned and waggled his brows, and she realized there could be some misinterpretation in her words.

"Uh..." Nori totally lost her train of thought. "To...to eat. Where did you want to go?"

Erik feigned disappointment then asked, "How about sushi? You know of a good place?"

Nori shuddered. Anything but sushi! "Well," she said hesitantly, "there is a place not far from here . . ." Atsushi had pointed it out one day when they were walking to the train, but—

"Well then, let's go." He held out his arm, and she slipped her hand into the crook of his elbow.

The sushi restaurant was the type of place Atsushi had called *kaitenzushi*. It featured a conveyor belt that ran throughout the restaurant. In the center, three white-clad sushi chefs shaped, stuffed, rolled, and cut sushi and sashimi at lightning speed and set plates of fresh offerings on the conveyor.

"If something comes along that you want to try," Nori told Erik, "just take it. They'll tally up what we owe at the end by counting the plates on the table." At least that's what she thought Atsushi had said. She glanced at the laminated menu taped to the table. "See, look." She pointed to the pictures on the menu. "The pink plates are three hundred yen, the green ones are four, and the blue ones are six."

Erik rubbed his hands together. "This is fantastic. I love sushi. What kind is your favorite?"

"Er…" Nori watched queasily as plates rolled past their table. She had absolutely no idea what any of them were. There were chunks of pink fish, white fish, even blue fish! And, ugh! Out of the top of one piece of rolled sushi waved a miniature tentacle, complete with tiny round suction cups. She thought she was going to be sick. "I like…" She snagged a plate with a couple of pieces of pink-and-white shrimp lying delicately atop slabs of rice. Shrimp was mild. "The *ebi* is good." She set the plate down in front of Erik.

"Oh, no," he said. "I can't take your favorite."

She forced a smile and picked up one piece with her chopsticks. "You have one, and I'll have one, how's that?"

She dipped it in her bowl of soy sauce and took a bite, trying valiantly not to pull a face. But then the sharp hotness of wasabi horseradish filled her mouth, bringing tears to her eyes and completely overpowering the taste of the shrimp. Aha. So that was the secret. Overpower the fish with wasabi.

Nori managed to share several plates of sushi with Erik by mixing liberal amounts of the green paste into her soy sauce. It killed the taste, but probably also the lining of her stomach.

"I'm full," she said when Erik offered her more. "You go ahead."

He grabbed a plate of rolled sushi with little ruby-colored round things piled on top of them. "Yes! Salmon roe!" He popped one into his mouth. "My favorite." He smiled, and she could see the little red balls stuck between his teeth.

She hid a grimace, stomach churning. So much for a romantic first date. "Wow, look at the time," she said. "We should go. I've got to finish my homework."

Valerivalera: Ha! Serves U right.

Revengelobster: Thanks so much.

Valerivalera: Anytime. Poetic justice, methinks.

Revengelobster: Then you'll love this—guess where we're going on Saturday?

Valerivalera: No idea.

Revengelobster: To a fish auction.

Valerivalera: ROTFL. MayB this is a sign. U bettr tell the boy the truth!

Actually, Nori was looking forward to her upcoming trek to the famous Tsukiji Fish Market. Not for the fish, of course, but because Erik would be her partner for the day.

When the morning arrived, Nori was up and ready long before the buses were scheduled, even though those buses would be hitting the road before five in the morning.

She couldn't ask Atsushi to help her out again; it was too soon since she had promised Akihabara would be the last time. Besides, she'd promised him that she would come clean with Erik. This one she was going to have to do solo.

Shouldn't be that hard to pull off. The fish market was one of those tourist destinations that was thoroughly reviewed and documented on the Internet. She'd read through a dozen commentaries and felt pretty confident. If she was vague enough, she might be able to bluff without Erik catching on that she had never actually been there before. If not, well, she'd have to figure out another way to "run into" Atsushi and let him do the talking.

Erik stumbled into the lobby, heavy-lidded eyes at half-mast, tawny hair mussed like a little boy's. Dang, even half asleep he looked hot.

He saw her standing by the door and raised his hand in

greeting, but before he could weave through the crowd of tired students to get to her, Michiko appeared at his side.

"*Ohayo gozaimasu*, Erik-*san*," she purred.

He smiled sleepily at Michiko in a way that made Nori's heart stop. Oh, no, you don't. She rushed forward. "Are you ready?"

It had the desired effect. Erik broke eye contact with Michiko and looked instead to Nori. His smile turned sheepish. She tried not to be too smug as they both turned their backs on Michiko.

Erik wasn't very talkative on the bus. In fact, he hardly said a word, but laid his head on her shoulder—which might have been romantic if he hadn't fallen asleep and started snoring. She enjoyed the contact as much as she could, though, and watched out the window as they rolled through the quiet Tokyo streets. When they arrived, she gave him a gentle shake to wake him.

He stumbled groggily beside her through the claustrophobic maze of market stalls toward the back building where the famed fish auction would take place. Motorized carts zipped through the aisles, and several times Nori had to pull Erik out of the way to keep him from getting run over.

The deeper they got into the market, the worse the smell became. Seriously, the place reeked! Which was not unexpected, since it was a fish market, but still. Good thing they hadn't had breakfast yet or she'd have totally hurled.

Even worse was when they waited in the auction room

and the men began dragging out the frozen tuna carcasses for bidding. The heads, tails, and fins had been chopped off so that the fish resembled frosty white torpedoes—except for when the workers hacked up a chunk of flesh in each one so that the buyers could judge the color and texture of the meat. It was all she could do to keep from getting sick right there on Erik's shoes.

After the "thrill" of the auction, the students were turned loose to wander through the stalls. Erik stuck close to Nori, which was the only thing that kept her from plotting an early escape back to the bus.

She feigned interest and pointed out trays of bright red octopi and spiky sea urchins. Many stalls featured bubbling glass-sided tanks containing live fish. Still more offered freshly cut samples for customers to try. Nori looked from one to the other and again felt her stomach turn.

Puddles of water and other slime she didn't even want to try to identify covered the concrete. Nori stepped gingerly over the worst of them. Kiah, however, was walking just ahead of them, the hem of her long jeans dragging through the muck, wicking up the moisture.

Nori grimaced. "Oh, that's just too gross."

Erik, on the other hand, found it amusing. "Wonder how long until she notices?"

"We should tell her."

"And spoil the fun?"

Nori pressed her lips together. Fun? Hardly. Still, she wasn't about to pull back when he took her hand and led her through the stalls, following Kiah and her absorbing jeans. He was actually holding her hand! Not that it was a conscious decision or anything. More like he was just hanging on to her so she wouldn't miss the show, but she'd take what she could get.

It wasn't until the moisture had darkened the fabric well above her ankles that Kiah glanced down. A look of horror spread across her face. She squealed and began pulling at her pant legs, lifting them away from her skin.

Erik's laughter boomed over the vendors' calls, and Kiah's head snapped in his direction. Her eyes met Nori's for an instant—long enough for Nori to read the dual message in her glare: Why didn't you tell me? and I hope you die a horrible death while the crocs and dingoes pick your bones clean.

Valerivalera: So, HH falls from the pedestal?

Revengelobster: Dunno. It just wasn't very nice.

Valerivalera: Unlike pretending to be someone U R NOT so that he'll like U? HELLOOOO?

Revengelobster: Am going to tell him.

Valerivalera: Right. When?

Revengelobster: Soon.

Valerivalera: Right.

Chapter Nine

Nori didn't tell Erik. She couldn't. Things were going too well to blow it now. Since Tsukiji, they had done something together every day—even if it was only to sit and talk. What a rush it was to see him walk into the room and look for her!

Atsushi had forgiven her for the slip in Akihabara, but things weren't quite the same between them. Though he still hung around, he was more like a guardian than a friend. He had an uncanny knack for showing up just when it looked like Erik was finally going to make a move. As far as Nori was concerned, Atsushi was taking the whole savior role a little too seriously. But it was her own fault, she supposed. After all, she was the one who got him involved in the first place. He was just looking out for her.

She could have used some looking out for in ecology. She was beginning to think that Nakamura-*sensei* had a mean streak a mile wide. How else could you explain the essay assignment he handed out the day before the term's first overnight trip?

"I expect you to put some real thought into your essays," he said. "What better place to consider the environment than in the ancient forests of Nikko?"

Nori groaned. Writing a paper was the last thing she wanted to be doing over the weekend. She was hoping to spend time with Erik and...Wait a minute. This just might turn out to be a good thing. Erik had written that brilliant essay in Nakamura-*sensei*'s class. He could easily help her come up with something.

Atsushi dropped into the seat in front of them just as Nori was about to ask Erik for help. She'd figured they would have plenty of time to talk about her paper on the long bus ride to Nikko.

"So," he said, twisting around to face them, "what are we talking about?"

"Ecology," Nori said. "I have to write a paper."

"Right. With Nakamura-*sensei*? Good luck."

"Wait. You're not taking his class, are you?"

He draped an arm over the seat back. "Naw. Had him before, though. I know how he operates."

"Oh, good. Then you can help me, too." She took Erik's hand. "I was just going to ask Erik for advice. His paper on reforestation was really good."

Erik shrugged. "It was nothing."

"Don't be so modest."

Atsushi pressed his lips together, conspicuously silent.

"What?" Nori asked.

"Nothing."

"No," Erik challenged. "If you have something to say, I want to hear it."

"All right, here it is. I read your essay, Erik. I will say it was well written, but...it wasn't original, and your thesis was a bit simplistic."

Uneasiness coiled in Nori's stomach. Underneath Atsushi's polite exterior ran an icy undercurrent. Where did that come from?

Erik stiffened, his grip on Nori's hand tightening. "Oh?"

"Well, yeah. It lacks depth. It's all about not dwelling on negatives, but the way I see it, if you don't address a problem, how are you going to come up with the solution?"

Erik's brow lowered. "You misunderstood my message."

Atsushi raised both hands in mock surrender. "Hey, I'm just saying. It might make your stance stronger if you broaden your perspective."

Anger flashed in Erik's blue eyes. "And you are an expert on broad perspectives, I suppose?"

"Look, forget about—"

Erik snorted and crossed his arms. "You are talking air."

Nori rubbed the circulation back into her fingers where Erik had been gripping them. "Wow," she said, "isn't that Mount Nantai? We should be—"

"I"—Erik tapped his chest—"have studied ecology and economics for the past three years. My perspective is adequately broad. On what do you base your lofty opinions?"

"Hey, I'm sorry I said anything. Let's move on."

"There is nothing worse than a coward who insults but will not defend his words."

Nori held her breath, but Atsushi just laughed. "Dude. Get over yourself."

"As I thought."

"Let it go."

Erik narrowed his eyes. "Admit it. You know nothing."

"Now wait a minute." Nori straightened.

Atsushi laid a hand on her arm. "It's okay. I've got this." His voice was uncannily calm. "Actually, Sussmann, I've studied for a lot longer than your three years. I've seen enough to recognize several problems and"—he raised a brow—"unlike some people who are all talk, I have tried to address them."

Erik stuck out his chin. "Oh, really. And what have you done?"

"At the moment I am designing a hybrid car that will not only slash emissions, but will be affordable to buy and to drive."

Erik's face registered shock. Nori closed her gaping jaw. "You design cars? I didn't know that."

Atsushi cut a glance at her, dark eyes intense. "There's a lot about me you don't know."

"But..." She blinked.

"My dad is in product development with Honda." Atsushi shrugged. "Guess he passed the car-obsession gene on to me."

"Sweet."

Erik didn't think so. "It is this obsession with cars that threatens our planet in the first place," he spat.

"And in keeping with your idea of jumping directly to a knee-jerk solution, what would you have us do?" Atsushi challenged. "Ban motorized transportation? How practical would that be? Look deeper at the problem, Sussmann. All we need is an alternative to what we already have."

"Like what?" Fascinated, Nori turned toward him. This was a side to Atsushi she hadn't seen before.

"Well..." His face lit up. "We need a better hybrid design. Something inexpensive to produce and to maintain. Something that can run on renewable resources. See, it isn't enough to talk about abstract solutions; we have to address the problems and think things through to their logical outcomes or we're just blowing hot air."

"Which would not be a good thing for global warming," Nori quipped.

Atsushi laughed, but a wave of chilly silence came from her right. Erik stared out the window like a petulant child.

"Maybe I should go sit somewhere else," Atsushi said in a low voice.

"No." Nori said, "Stay."

"I think it would be better if I didn't."

He stood and walked down the aisle. She watched his back, a weird sort of confusion twisting inside. Turning to Erik, she snapped, "What's the matter with you? Atsushi is my friend!"

"Nori-*chan*..." He took her hand.

She pulled it away. "I'm serious. You were a real jerk just now."

Erik had the grace to look remorseful. "I am sorry. I didn't mean to be...a jerk." It almost sounded comical with his German accent. He reached for her hand again. "Forgive me." His thumb stroked her palm in lazy circles, trailing heat. Her mouth went dry.

"You should apologize to him," she managed.

"I promise I will," he said.

But by the time they got off the bus for a pit stop at Lake Chuzenji, the argument was forgotten and things were back to normal.

Except that Atsushi was no longer with them.

Erik took Nori's hand. "Come, let's walk by the water."

They strolled down a grassy hillside and stood near a dock where a herd of swan-shaped paddleboats gathered like the starting lineup of a Disney parade.

"It's beautiful, is it not?" Erik said, draping his arm around her shoulders.

She rested her head against his solid biceps, deciding just to enjoy the moment. "Mmm-hmmm. Beautiful." She looked out over the sapphire water with its mirrored images of trees and spun-sugar clouds. It was like standing in a fairy tale.

Sensing his eyes on her, she glanced up to find Erik looking at her strangely. "What?"

"This is how I will always remember you," he said. "Beauty surrounded by beauty."

She giggled. Giggled! Immediately, she clamped her hand over her mouth. What was that? She never giggled. What, was she turning into Amberly or something? Let a guy spout a corny line and she starts getting all giddy?

Erik's arm tightened around her shoulders. He leaned closer, eyes half closed. Her breath caught. He was going to kiss her! She let her hand drop. She couldn't have asked for a more romantic spot for a first kiss. It was perfect.

Until he whispered, "My beautiful geisha."

What was his fixation with geisha? "Erik, I really wish you wouldn't say—"

"Hey, no pashing at the lake!"

Nori jumped and twisted around to find Kiah and Amberly walking toward them with Teruo and Yoshi. "We're not doing anything," she blurted, and then felt totally stupid for saying so.

The girls exchanged wry looks.

"Well, don't let us interrupt you," Kiah said. "We'll let you get back to…doing nothing."

They strolled on down the path, leaving Nori and Erik alone once more. But Erik made no further moves. The moment, whatever it was, had passed.

When they got back on the bus, Nori noticed that Atsushi was sitting in the back with Michiko and her friends. Even though she knew it shouldn't have bothered her, it did. She sat quietly next to Erik, a surge of conflicting thoughts swirling inside her head. Atsushi was just a friend. He was entitled to hang out with whomever he wanted. She wasn't asking his permission to be with Erik, was she?

Erik, who almost kissed her. But didn't.

She kept replaying the argument from earlier. Erik really had acted like a jerk, but Atsushi had started it, hadn't he? Or did she start it by gushing about Erik's paper in the first place? The entire thing was just weird.

And then there was that whole "There's a lot you don't know about me," from Atsushi. What was that?

Of course, he was right. She'd never given him much of a chance to talk about himself when they were together. But why should she care? She got what she wanted, right? Erik was hers. So what was her problem?

She resolved to find out. As soon as they got to the inn, she would talk to Atsushi.

But that wasn't the way it worked. Accommodations that night were divided between two traditional Japanese hot-spring inns, nestled deep in a shaded forest. The girls stayed at one inn and the guys at another. Nori's talk with Atsushi would have to wait.

Ms. Jameson gathered the girls in the lobby of their inn. "Please be respectful of the other guests," she reminded them. "The purpose of this visit is to experience Japanese culture, not to disrupt it."

She divided them into groups of six and passed out room assignments. Nori and Amberly joined Kiah and Kirsti and two other girls from their floor at the dorms. Kikuchi-*san* showed them to their room.

"We're going to fit six people in here?" Amberly whispered, eyeing the small, square room with its white paneled walls and woven straw tatami floor. Along one wall were sliding shoji doors that hid the minuscule closets and futon storage. And that was it.

"No worries," said Kiah, kicking off her shoes at the door and stepping inside. "Three on that side and three on this. Piece of cake."

"You girls will be first at the *onsen*," Kikuchi-*san* said. "Please bring your *yukata* and follow me."

Yes. An *onsen* was a natural hot-springs pool. Nori had

been waiting for this all term, ever since she read about the outing in the student packet. She grabbed her towel, swimsuit, and the thin, cotton robe provided by the inn and padded off behind the group.

She'd been to hot springs before. On a vacation to Colorado, her family had soaked in the mineral waters of Yampah in Glenwood Springs. In their swimming suits. So she was totally unprepared for what came next.

Kikuchi-*san* led them to a dressing room with narrow lockers and a bench down the center. "You will leave your clothing in these lockers," she said. "In the *onsen* room please take a bucket. You fill with water to wash yourself. Use the ladle to rinse. Please wash and rinse thoroughly before stepping into the pool."

Nori's eyes widened in horror as she looked from Kikuchi-*san* to her group. "We're bathing? Together? I don't think so."

"Oh, don't be so prudish," said Kirsti.

"Cut her some slack," Kiah said, hanging her shirt in her locker. "You're used to taking sauna in the nuddie. This might be out of her comfort zone."

Um, yeah.

Eyes downcast, Nori undressed and wrapped a towel tightly around herself before following the group. She stood self-consciously on the wooden slats that covered the entry and bathing areas and looked around the room. Along one wall protruded several spigots where they were to wash.

Near each was a low wooden stool, a bucket, and a ladle. The rest of the room consisted of three steaming pools, complete with gentle rock waterfalls and carefully tended landscaping. The place smelled musty but clean, like a forest after rain. And it looked inviting enough...

As she waited for her turn to wash, she noticed two withered old ladies crouched on stools near the corner, naked as the day they were born. They were chatting casually as they ladled water over each other's knobby back, not the least bit shy about letting it all hang out in front of everyone else in the room. Or hang down, as the case may be.

If they could do it she could, too. As a compromise, Nori draped her towel over her back and she faced the wall to wash, and then held the towel around herself until she reached the edge of the pool, letting it drop only when she could quickly slip into the water. She sighed in pleasure as the heat closed around her body.

The old ladies climbed into the pool next to hers, continuing their conversation with much hand gesturing and quiet laughter. Nori watched them without realizing she was staring. They seemed so happy, so comfortable, so sure of themselves. Nori wondered how it would feel to be like that.

One day she hoped to find out.

Chapter Ten

In the morning, the students met up in the parking lot near the Toshogu Shrine. Nori shouldered her backpack and went looking for Atsushi. Her stomach dropped when she saw him. He was with Michiko at the far side of the parking lot. The two of them were laughing about something. Michiko swatted Atsushi's shoulder playfully and tossed her raven hair like she was in a shampoo commercial. Yeesh! She was so obvious. It's a wonder Atsushi couldn't see right through it.

She stiffened. What if Michiko was playing him like Erik? After what she had learned on the bus yesterday, Nori fig-

ured Atsushi could be a front-runner for the scholarship, too. Was that why Michiko kept hanging around? Should she say something?

"There you are." Erik sidled up to her and slid his arm around her shoulders, steering her toward the huge *torii* gates at the shrine's entrance. "Come. Tell me about this place."

Nori tore her gaze from Atsushi and Michiko. She looked up at Erik. Lost herself in those blue eyes. Decided Atsushi was a big boy and could take care of himself. "Let's catch up with the class," she said. "Wada-*sensei* knows all the stories and dates and details I might have forgotten."

Amberly's voice rang out behind her. "Forgotten? From when?"

Erik turned his dazzling smile on her. "Ah, good morning. Would you care to join us?" he asked, holding out his arm.

"Well…" She glanced behind to where Teruo and Yoshi stood. She beckoned with her chin for them to follow and, with a sideways glance at Nori, said, "Sure. This should be interesting."

They joined the group of students trailing Wada-*sensei*. As Nori had hoped, he kept up a running commentary, so she didn't have to say anything to reveal her ignorance.

"This complex is recognized for its fascinating blend of Shinto and Buddhist elements," Wada-*sensei* said. "Notice the extensive use of gold leaf and carvings on the buildings.

You won't see this much anywhere else in Japan since, traditionally, shrines are known for their simplicity."

These buildings were anything but simple. Each one featured intricate carvings, brightly painted. The artists must have liked dragons, cats, and monkeys the most, because those creatures appeared over and over again.

When the class reached a building called the Sacred Stable, Nori immediately zeroed in on a carving of three monkeys, hands covering their mouth, eyes, or ears respectively. "Hear no evil, see no evil, speak no evil!" Nori just about blurted out her recognition but caught herself in time. Cool. Be cool. She turned casually to Erik and asked, "Are you familiar with this carving?"

Amberly sure was. She gasped. "Hey, I've seen this before! I didn't know they came from here."

Nori nodded and smiled indulgently as if it were common knowledge.

By lunchtime, Amberly, who had apparently not found Nori and Erik's company to be as interesting as she'd hoped, drifted away, well accompanied by her band of groupies.

"Would you like me to get the lunch boxes?" Erik asked.

"That would be nice. Thank you." As Erik jogged down the path, Nori sank onto a bench in the shade of the cypress boughs and bent over her notebook, trying to outline her paper for ecology. Here, in the midst of the trees, reforestation came to mind, but that was what Erik had written about.

She needed something new. Something meaningful to her.

"You alone?" Atsushi stood before her, hands dug deep into his jeans pockets.

"Yeah." Nori glanced down the path. "What's up?"

He shrugged. "Not much."

"I can see that."

Atsushi cleared his throat. "Listen, Nori. There's something I need to talk to you about—"

"Yeah, I wanted to ask you something, too."

"You go first."

"No, you."

"Okay. Well..." He dug the toe of his Nike in the dirt and looked away. "I'm saying this friend to friend, all right?"

Nori's gut tightened. It was never going to be good when someone started off like that. "Go on."

"It's Erik—"

She slapped her notebook shut. "I knew it! What is it with you guys, anyway?"

He ran a hand through his hair, making it stand up in little blond-tipped spikes. He blew out a breath. "It's just... he's not the genuine article, you know?"

"No, I don't know."

"Come on. He's got all the sincerity of a used-car salesman."

"Hey, I know you don't like him, but—"

"Just think about taking a step back, okay?"

"You've got to be kidding me."

"Dead serious."

"Atsushi—"

"*Konnichiwa.*" Erik strolled up, holding two *o-bento* boxes. "Looks like I should have grabbed another lunch."

"No." Atsushi stepped back, banging his fist against his leg. "I was just leaving."

Nori shook her head. "You can stay."

He bowed farewell. "We'll talk later," he said. And then he was gone.

Nori turned in her ecology paper with a little twinge of regret. She knew it was not her best work, but the weekend had not gone quite as she had planned. The whole thing with Atsushi was just so weird that she found it hard to concentrate on anything else. Besides, she had hoped to get Erik's input, but every time she tried to talk to him about it, he steered the conversation in a different direction. Nori was surprised. He had written about the environment so passionately in his paper. Where was his passion now?

When she tried to bring it up at lunch, Erik just shrugged and looked away. "That is only one aspect of who I am, Nori."

"Well, yes, I know that, but—"

He stood and held his hand out to her. "Let's get to class. We don't want to be late."

As they approached the classroom, Nori saw Atsushi standing near the door. She quickly dropped Erik's hand, feeling inexplicably guilty. She murmured a hello and man-

aged a smile, but he didn't smile back. She could feel his eyes on her all the way to her desk.

Wada-*sensei* strode into the room, signaling for everyone to take their seats. When they were all settled, he smiled and asked, "Are there any lovers in the room?"

Nori almost swallowed her gum. Yeah. I wish.

Wada-*sensei* turned to the blackboard and scrawled the words *Star-Crossed Lovers.* "Who," he said over his shoulder, "knows anything about *Tanabata?*"

Michiko's hand shot up. "It is the festival celebrating the stars Vega and her lover, Altair," she said loftily. "They fell in love and began neglecting their work. This angered the emperor, who placed the Milky Way between them to keep them apart. The only time they can see each other is on the night of *Tanabata,* when they cross a bridge of magpies' wings. That is why it is also called the lovers' festival." She glanced meaningfully at Erik, who didn't seem to notice.

Nori did, however, and had a sudden urge to go pull out a good chunk of Michiko's hair.

"That's right," Wada-*sensei* said. He picked up a pile of colored paper strips from his desk. "On Thursday we will be attending the *Tanabata* Festival in Hiratsuka." Dumping a handful of strips on the first desk of each row, he instructed the students to take a few and pass the rest back. "In preparation, we will be making our own *Tanabata* decorations for the room. This is *tanzaku* paper, upon which you may write your wishes. Legend has it that if you tie your *tanzaku* wishes on the bamboo tree, they will come true."

The rest of the class was just a blur. All Nori could think about was the lovers' festival. She knew exactly what wish she was going to write on her *tanzaku*.

Hiratsuka station was just over an hour away from Shinjuku. Nori spent the entire ride that Thursday in breathless anticipation. This was the night. It had to be. She'd done everything she could to make it happen: let Amberly choose her outfit, wore just enough lip gloss, even avoided Atsushi so that she and Erik could be alone long enough for him to kiss her.

Well, as alone as possible.

Because of the crowds and the nature of the festival, Wada-*sensei* had decreed that the class should try to stay together. He walked in front, holding high a long stick with a red handkerchief stapled to the top. "If you lose the group," he said, "just look for the flag."

He led the way to the station exit, raising his voice above the buzz of the crowd. "Each year this city transforms itself," he said. "They close three major streets and fill about ten acres with festivities and decorations."

Nori could hear the music of those festivities before they even reached the turnstiles. Walking out of the station, she drew in a delighted gasp. The entire block was lined with decorated bamboo poles angled over the streets. Streamers

and *tanzaku* papers fluttered in the breeze. Storefronts and light poles had been turned into showcases, some with animated displays. Hundreds of people milled about, many of them dressed in colorful *yukata*.

Erik tugged on Nori's hand. "Let's lose this group," he said.

She flashed him her most alluring smile. "Why, Erik—"

"I want to try some of those octopus balls from that cart over there. I heard they're really good. You want some?"

Um, no. "You go ahead," she said. "I'll be right over here." She pointed to a vendor selling long strips of colored paper. "I need to fill out another *tanzaku*."

Valerivalera: So did it work?

Revengelobster: Hardly.

Valerivalera: Nothing?

Revengelobster: Not a pucker.

Valerivalera: What's wrong with that boy?

Revengelobster: I know. I mean, really.

Valerivalera: So what did U do at the festival?

Revengelobster: Shop, eat, ooh and aah at the decorations.

Valerivalera: And U leave for Kyoto when?

Revengelobster: Saturday.

Valerivalera: 4 how long?

REVENGELOBSTER: A week.

Valerivalera: This is getting serious. Gotta pull out all the stops, girlfriend. Here's what you do...

Chapter Eleven

Guys are so predictable. Never in a million years would Nori have believed Val's suggestion would work, but here she was, standing in the shadows of the hallway with Erik, and she had him totally eating out of her hand.

She looked up at him from under her lashes, pouting. For the record, Nori truly hated pouty girls. Under normal circumstances, she would never have stooped so low as to play the pout card, but the situation was getting desperate. She would be leaving in the morning, and she didn't want Erik to forget about her while she was gone.

His face crumpled. "You are going away?"

Nori sniffed tragically. "It's my mother. She insists I spend the home stay with relatives in Kyoto."

"I am so very sorry to hear that." Erik pulled her to him and stroked her hair like a little child.

She closed her eyes and laid her head on his chest, enjoying the feel of him and the smell of him and...wait. What *was* that smell? More octopus balls? Ugh! She coughed. "I wish I didn't have to go," she said.

Erik suddenly pulled back, holding her at arm's length. "We will need a...what do you call it? A send-off?" His blue eyes were alight with more enthusiasm than she had seen the entire term. "Tonight. After the counselors have gone to bed. We'll go out together."

"Uh..."

"My Nori-*chan*." He fingered a length of her hair. "This is your last night. We must spend it together."

Well, that was romantic. But after curfew? "What if we get locked out?"

"They do not lock the doors. I have noticed the university students come in very late."

She furrowed her brows. When would he have noticed that? "But—"

He placed a finger on her lips. The touch sent sparks down to her toenails. "Hush," he said—as if she could have uttered a word just then—"it will be all right. Trust me."

Trust. Yikes. "Well..."

He clasped his hands behind her back, drawing her close

again. He leaned down so that his face was right next to hers. Easily within kissing distance. Maybe this was it. Nori tilted her head back a fraction and relaxed her lips, just in case. "Come on." His breath caressed her cheek. "Show me how the Japanese have fun."

Well.

Now, that could mean anything.

"Um...what do you have in mind?"

He flashed his white teeth in a triumphant smile. "That is the Nori I know." He toyed with her hair some more. "Show me the Tokyo nightlife. We'll go to some clubs."

She swallowed. Right. Like I know any. And after curfew? If they got caught, they could be sent home. That would sit real well with her mom and dad. This really was not a good idea. Still, Erik seemed so confident...She smiled up at him. "Whatever you say."

Nori considered her options. Amberly shouldn't be too much of a problem since she went to bed by ten every night— beauty sleep and all that. But the fact that Nori actually knew of no nightclubs anywhere nearby? That might just present a major obstacle. Maybe she could find some decent clubs online. Ones that were close to the train stations so she wouldn't get lost.

What would she wear? She hadn't packed in anticipation of going clubbing. Not that she would have known what to pack if she had. What was the look for a Tokyo nightclub,

anyway? Trendy? Funky? Amberly could hardly help her put something together this time. She pawed through her clothes in disgust. Everything she owned screamed mid-western schoolgirl. All right, so she was a midwestern schoolgirl, but tonight she didn't want to look like one.

What would Val wear? She smiled at a memory of Val pulling a pair of black pants from the shelf at Abercrombie. "When in doubt, wear black," she'd said. Digging through the pile again, Nori selected the cropped pants she'd never worn and a black knit tee and laid them carefully aside. She'd change once Amberly was asleep.

When Amberly entered the room, Nori plugged into her iPod and did her best to ignore her. Without an audience to listen to her review the day, Amberly might tire of her calligraphy early and crawl off to bed.

It didn't work. In fact, Amberly was still going strong at quarter past ten—just forty-five minutes before Erik would be waiting in the lobby.

Nori stood and stretched her arms up over her head. "Wow. It's past bedtime," she said, yawning. "Boy, am I tired."

Amberly glanced up. "I'm just going to finish up here," she said. "I'll try to be quiet so you can sleep."

Nori groaned inwardly. No! Go to bed now! She sauntered over to Amberly's desk and asked casually, "How much more do you have to do?"

Amberly quickly slid some of her papers into a large portfolio. "It's for my presentation," she said guardedly. "I don't want to show anyone until I'm done."

"Oh. Okay." Nori hovered anyway, sending out you-are-getting-sleepy vibes. "This is new," she said, picking up a black-and-gold flower vase. The water sloshed a little and the arrangement of red gerberas tilted to the side.

"Got it this afternoon," Amberly said. She took the vase from Nori's hands and set it back on the desk, wiping off the moisture and straightening the flowers. "The room needed a little brightening up, don't you think?"

Whatever. "You almost done?"

Amberly set down her brush. "Listen, I don't mean to be rude, but I can't work when anyone's watching. Would you mind?"

"Oh. Sorry."

Nori made a big show of getting out her futon, fluffing her pillow, putting on her nightshirt. Amberly was too intent on her work to pay any attention. Nori glanced at her watch. Ten thirty. Hurry up! She lay down and pretended to sleep.

Finally, about quarter to eleven, Amberly stood. She gathered her brushes and tiptoed to the door. Nori knew the routine. Amberly would spend the next ten minutes rinsing the things in the bathroom sink before laying them carefully on the desk to dry. Nori rushed to the closet and pulled out her clothes. She changed quickly and then scrambled back under the covers, pulling the quilt up to her chin.

By the time Amberly cleaned her desk, set up her futon, turned out the lights, and lay down to sleep, it was nearly eleven. Erik would be waiting. What if he thought Nori was standing him up? He would wait for her, wouldn't he? Of course he would. If nothing else, Erik was a gentleman. She counted the minutes until she heard Amberly's breath settle into a rhythmic pattern.

"Amberly," she whispered, "are you awake?" No answer. Good. Hard as it was to do so, Nori waited a couple more minutes for good measure before tiptoeing to the door.

Amberly sighed in her sleep and the blankets rustled as she rolled over. Nori paused, stomach tight. Maybe she shouldn't do this. What if they got caught? On the other hand, what about Erik? She was leaving tomorrow. This might be their night. She couldn't blow it.

Carrying her shoes so they wouldn't click against the tiled floor, she tiptoed down the hallway. A quick peek at her reflection in the steel elevator doors told her that Val's fashion advice was right on. Black made her look more sophisticated. A little...daring.

Only she didn't feel daring; she felt sick.

On the ride down, she pulled out her mirror with trembling fingers and applied extra mascara and lip gloss. Deep breaths, she told herself. It will be all right. As she was putting the cosmetics back in her purse, she noticed the little black velvet bag with the jade pendant. Slipping the silk cord over her head, she rubbed her fingers over the smooth carving. She was going to need all the luck she could get.

When Erik saw her, his eyes lit up. He gave her the up and down and smiled approvingly. "I thought you might not come," he whispered, slipping his arm around her waist.

Nori hoped he wouldn't feel the little tremors of nervousness running through her body as she returned his smile. "I wouldn't miss this for the world," she said. "Come on." She tugged on his hand and led him from the lobby.

All the way to the train station, she prayed that she'd remember the way to get to where they were going. Though she had printed out a subway map and the directions to three nightclubs whose Web sites looked cool—and had English Web pages—she could hardly whip those out now. She was supposed to know Tokyo. Know these clubs.

Luckily, Gaspanic 99 was located very near Roppongi station on the Oedo Line, so all she had to do was get them on the right train, and they arrived without incident.

Erik took charge once they were inside the door, grabbing Nori's hand and leading her through the darkness and strobing lights to a table in the back. Heavy bass music thrummed in her head. Cigarette smoke filled her nostrils. She shuddered.

He gave her a questioning look.

"I…uh…I love this song," she shouted over the noise. "It gives me chills."

He scooted his chair closer to hers and placed his hand on her back, leaning closer. "What?"

The heat of his hand burned through her thin T-shirt. She swallowed drily. "This song," she croaked. "I love it."

"Who is the band?"

Her smile froze. She didn't know any Japanese groups. But then, most likely, neither did he. "Wazaki," she said, picking a random word out of the air. In fact, she wasn't even sure it was a word.

"Who?"

"Wazaki. Have you heard of them?"

"They sound like that British band, The Rakes."

Snap! No wonder it sounded familiar. "Yes, I think Wazaki was heavily influenced by The Rakes."

"What?"

"Let's get something to drink." She waved to the waitress to get her attention. "Cola, *futatsu*," she called, holding up two fingers in case she'd said it wrong. The waitress nodded and disappeared into the crowd.

When she returned, she placed two empty glasses on the table, followed by two open bottles of Corona beer.

Nori blanched. "Oh, *sumimasen*. This is not—" But the waitress only bowed and walked away.

Erik filled the glasses, eyeing the suds as they neared the rim. She stared at him, chin dropping. He didn't think she was going to drink that, did he? She had never had beer in her life. Or any alcohol for that matter. Her parents would totally freak. Of course, her parents weren't here...

Oblivious, Erik placed the full beer glass in her hand. "To us," he said, and clinked the rim of his glass on hers.

Well, how could she not drink to that? Maybe just a little sip wouldn't hurt. She pressed the glass to her lips, wrinkling her nose at the fermented smell. It reminded her of rotten fruit. She took a sip. Aagh! It tasted even worse. She managed a smile, but set her glass down, relatively untouched.

Erik completely drained his.

"You like that stuff?" she asked.

He shrugged. "It is not as rich as German beer." But he must have found it palatable, because when the waitress passed the table, Erik held up his empty glass, gesturing for another.

For over an hour they sat in the noisy, smoke-filled club, barely talking to each other because it was too hard to hear over the music. Erik drank another Corona before switching to Kirin "to experience the culture." Nori didn't want to appear unsophisticated, but the combination of a guilty conscience, a virgin stomach, and the smoky atmosphere was making her feel sick.

Finally she couldn't stand it any longer.

"We should go," she said. Without waiting for an answer, she plonked some yen down on the table, stood, and wove her way to the front of the club.

In the open air, she coughed to clear her lungs of the foulness from inside. This was so not her scene.

Erik sauntered out moments later, flushed from the alcohol and looking particularly loose-jointed. "Where next?" he asked.

"I think we should go back to the dorms now," Nori said, voice trembling.

He froze. "Back? But the evening has just started."

"Um, I'm not feeling very well," she said. And that was the honest truth, for once.

"So we will walk for a while. You will feel better soon." He put his arm around her and tried to steer her back to the club.

She pulled away. "No. I mean it. We should go home. Right now."

The smile left his face. "I do not wish to return."

"Well, I do." She spun around and stalked to the station. If someone tells you she isn't feeling well, you take her home. Period.

Erik followed a few steps behind. "Nori." His voice took on a wheedling tone. "Go with me."

Nori stopped at the station doors, staring up at the train schedule, the beer in her stomach beginning to curdle.

They weren't going anywhere.

The last train back to Shinjuku had left ten minutes ago.

Chapter Twelve

It took all the rest of the money Nori had with her for the taxi fare back to the dorms. She wasn't about to ask Erik to pitch in since she was the one insisting that they go home. Of course, what would he have done if he'd stayed behind? The trains didn't start running again until five. Had he been planning to stay out all night?

She hugged the door all the way to the dorms while he stared out the window. She'd blown it with him, she was sure. Maybe she should have just pretended to be having a good time. Maybe they should have tried another club. Maybe—

The cab pulled up outside the dormitory. Erik took Nori's hand to help her out. And he didn't let go. She glanced up at his face. Was everything okay, then?

"Shhh," he said as they entered the silent lobby. "Ms. Jameson's room is right down the hall."

Nori nodded and allowed Erik to lead her to the elevator. The bell chimed as the door slid open; Erik turned to her, miming a horrified reaction to the sound. She couldn't help but giggle as he led her into the elevator.

He leaned against the wall and pulled her to him. "I will miss you," he said.

She tentatively rested her cheek against his chest. His heart thrummed in her ear.

"Nori," he said. "My little geisha."

She stiffened and pulled away. "Stop calling me that."

The elevator reached Erik's floor. As the doors slid open, he pulled her against him again.

"Sayonara," he whispered, and planted a wet one right on her lips.

Really wet. Slobbery, actually.

Nori's heart dropped. This wasn't exactly what she had hoped for in a first kiss. His breath reeked, his lips were clammy, and hers were bruised up against her teeth. When he pulled away, she had to suppress a powerful urge to wipe off her mouth.

He let go of her and stepped off the elevator into the deserted hallway.

Or maybe not quite so deserted. Behind Erik someone stepped out of the shadows.

Atsushi's dark eyes met hers, disappointment written in his drawn brows and the downward tug on his lips.

"Atsushi, I—"

He shook his head. The doors slid shut.

Nori's stomach, which wasn't doing so great in the first place, twisted and churned. She reached up to press the open-door button. She should talk to him. Explain. She paused. Yeah, explain what? He saw what he saw, and it was exactly what it looked like.

She banged her head back against the cold elevator paneling and rode to her floor in a miserable haze. Of all the things that had just happened, that look in Atsushi's eyes bothered her the most.

Nori slipped off her shoes and padded barefoot to her room. She eased the door open and slipped inside. Tiptoed to the closet and gently rolled the door back.

"It's okay. I'm awake."

She spun around, heart tripping. Amberly sat cross-legged on her futon, silhouetted by the moonlight from the window. Nori couldn't see her face, but she could hear the reproach in her voice.

"Do you have any idea what time it is?"

Nori swallowed. "What are you, my mother?"

"Where were you?"

"Out." She turned her back on Amberly and started to get

ready for bed. She pulled her shirt off over her head. It stank of cigarette smoke.

Amberly waited until she was done. "I was really worried about you," she said. "Why didn't you say you were going out? I wouldn't have told."

Biting her tongue, Nori gathered her toothbrush, towel, and face soap and stalked toward the door. She was so not in the mood for an inquisition.

"Were you with Erik?" Amberly continued, voice tight.

"You know what? I really don't need this right now."

"What you need is for someone to tell it like it is, Nori. You're not good with him. Not yourself."

Nori laughed humorlessly. "Not myself? You have no idea what my self is."

"I know you're not what you're acting like. And you've been using Atsushi—"

"Leave him out of it."

"Yeah, that's exactly what you should have done."

A barb of guilt twisted in Nori's gut. Amberly was right. And that only made Nori angrier. "Enough already!" she hissed, swinging around to face Amberly.

Ploink!

The sound stunned Nori for a second before she realized what it was. Her anger was quickly overcome by remorse. "Oh, oh! I'm so sorry!" She rushed to turn on the light.

It was even worse than she'd imagined. Water covered the

desk. Flowers splayed across several curling pieces of paper where Amberly's hard work was dissolving into black rivulets that ran down the paper and dropped—*splat, splat, splat*—onto the floor.

"I must have knocked it over with my towel," Nori murmured. "I am so, so sorry."

Without a word, Amberly crawled over and helped Nori mop up the mess. She gathered the sodden papers and stared at them for a long time.

Nori looked over her shoulder. The papers were completely unsalvageable. But the kanji she could still see were really very good. The strokes were executed so smoothly the characters looked like they could leap from the page. "Oh, Amberly. All your beautiful calligraphy."

Amberly nodded.

"I'm so sorry," Nori offered again.

"It's okay. They weren't any good anyway."

"Of course they were," Nori said awkwardly. "You... you're really talented."

Amberly gave her a sad smile. "You don't have to say that," she said. "I know I'm not. I just had to have something to do for a project, you know? Not like it's my life's dream or anything."

"No. You really are good at this."

"Really?" Amberly looked to Nori, eyes glistening with tears. Man, way to make you feel like a total heel.

"Really," Nori said, and she was surprised to find that she meant it.

Sleep was impossible. What a mess she'd made of everything! Amberly was completely right, of course. She hadn't been thinking of anyone but herself ever since the day she got here. Her first taste of freedom and what did she do with it? Maybe her mom was right to micromanage every little thing she did. She was obviously too much of an idiot to be left alone.

She pulled out her journal, squinting in the darkness to scrawl her thoughts.

> Things I wish I could change:
> I wouldn't have lied to Erik.
> I wouldn't have used Atsushi.
> I wouldn't have snuck out.
> I wouldn't have been such a troll to Amberly.

It didn't make her feel much better. She lay awake until dawn, an indescribable ache in her chest. Maybe it would have been better if she'd never come to Japan in the first place.

The next morning, Amberly acted as if nothing had happened the night before, which only made Nori feel worse.

How could she still be so nice? She helped Nori pack her suitcase and even rode all the way to Tokyo station, where Nori would catch the bullet train to Kyoto.

"I'll take pictures of everything that happens this week," Amberly said. "That way you won't really be missing anything."

"Thanks," Nori managed, knowing she didn't deserve any special consideration.

When the train pulled up, Amberly gave her a quick hug. "Have fun!" she said.

She waved good-bye as the train pulled out, and Nori could swear those were real tears in her eyes.

Erik did not come to say good-bye, though.

Neither did Atsushi.

Nori leaned back against the seat, watching the Japanese countryside zip by. High-rises gave way to homes, and homes gave way to rice paddies, rolling hills, and feathery bamboo forests. Off in the distance, white-capped Mount Fuji rose like a sentinel over the Kanto Plain. Any other time, Nori might have appreciated the beauty of it all.

She glanced around at the other passengers in the bullet train's crowded car. Even in the midst of all these people, she'd never felt so alone in her life.

Chapter Thirteen

The rhythm of the train must have lulled her into a much-needed sleep because the next thing Nori knew, the conductor was announcing Kyoto as the next stop. She glanced anxiously out the window to see the scenery moving past at a slower pace. Her stomach began to hurt. What if she made as big a mess of things in Kyoto as she had in Tokyo?

Reluctantly, she slipped her journal and iPod into her backpack and gathered her things. "Here goes nothing," she muttered.

• • •

The Kyoto station felt larger than Shinjuku, but not nearly as crazy. Still, the platform was crowded, and a quick stab of panic shot through her. What if she couldn't find her aunt and uncle? What if they forgot about her? What if they changed their minds?

But then she saw them. An old gray-haired couple watching the train, holding a sign written in big block letters that said WELCOME NORI! He was wearing a tucked-in Hawaiian-print shirt and white tennis shoes with his dress slacks, and she was neatly put together in an A-line tan skirt and a cream-colored blouse.

Though Nori was sure she'd never seen them before, there was something familiar about them. The man had a kind, round face just like her grandfather. He wore a Gilligan hat, which he removed to swipe his balding head with a handkerchief. He bent to say something to the woman, whose smile reached all the way up to her crinkly eyes. She reached up to tuck a stray hair into her neat French twist and continued to scan the passengers.

Nori gathered what little courage she could find and approached them. "*Konnichiwa*," she said with more confidence than she felt. "*Watashi wa Nori desu.*"

The man bowed in greeting and said, "It is good to meet you, Nori-*chan*. I am your great-uncle Kentaro, and this is your great-aunt Rika. You must call us 'Baba' and 'Jiji.' They are fond nicknames for 'grandmother' and 'grandfather.'"

Aunt Rika pointed to herself and said, "Baba." Again, she smiled with those eyes—eyes so dark that you couldn't tell where the pupils ended and the irises began.

Nori repeated the word and was rewarded with an even deeper bow. She looked shyly at Uncle Kentaro and said, "Jiji?"

He smiled his approval as he picked up Nori's suitcase and led the way from the station to the bicycle parking lot. "Never felt the need for a car," he explained.

They had brought an extra bike for Nori—a utilitarian thing, with a clunky seat and faded blue paint. Just the sort of bike she would not have been caught dead riding back home. Home. Just thinking of it was like a knife in the gut. Mom alone in her king-sized bed, Dad off in some matchbox apartment two towns away. She wondered if Baba and Jiji knew he had moved out.

"Come," Jiji said as he swept up her suitcase and balanced it across his handlebars. They took turns with the suitcase as they wound their way through the streets of Kyoto. Nori panted in the heat as she struggled to keep up.

Jiji led them down a narrow road lined with modern glass-and-steel businesses. Right smack in the middle of the block stood a tall brick wall with a round gate. It was a sight Nori had grown accustomed to in Tokyo. When the cities expanded, they grew around the shrines and temples. She imagined this charming wall surrounded such a place.

But then Jiji announced, "We are home."

Nori raised her brows. "This is where you live?"

Jiji smiled proudly as he unlocked the gate. "*Hai*. It is."

Inside the entry gate it was like another world. Every centimeter of the yard was laid out with container plants, rock formations, and perennials. Just how Nori had imagined a samurai's garden to be. On either side of the shed where they parked their bikes stood two gnarly pines with foliage pruned into rounded tufts. A haunting, hollow sound rose from the bamboo wind chime hanging from a red-leafed maple.

"It's perfect," she breathed.

Jiji chuckled. "*Domo arigato*, Nori-*chan*. I am pleased you like it."

As Jiji secured the shed, Baba led Nori up the pebble walkway to a house with smooth stucco walls beneath the swooping gables of a blue ceramic-tile roof. "Welcome to our home," she said in gentle, halting English.

Standing in the step-down entryway, Nori could smell an old-house mustiness beneath the peppery straw of the woven tatami mats. The rice-paper sliding doors had yellowed, and the painted scroll hanging in the little niche in the front hall looked brittle.

"Please, you will remove your shoes here," Baba said. She stepped out of hers and lined them up neatly facing outward. Nori did the same, wincing at the size of her shoes in comparison to Baba's tiny ones. Baba had laid out a pair of slippers for her. "Wear indoors to protect tatami floors," she explained.

Nori had a room to herself. Against one wall was a recessed platform that almost looked like a shrine except that there was a flower arrangement and another painted scroll there instead of an idol or something. Her window had a thin film over the glass made to look like rice paper. Baba opened one side.

"Here, Nori-*chan*. You can see Jiji's garden."

Nori peered out the window. A little stone pagoda and a collection of bonsai trees surrounded the lily-filled koi pond, complete with a graceful arching footbridge. Under a bent Japanese maple sat a bench where Nori could imagine spending a lot of time just thinking.

"I leave you to privacy," Baba said. "You rest. We eat soon."

Nori sat by the window and rested her chin on the sill. Even though she hadn't wanted to come, Nori felt strangely comfortable here already. Like she'd come home.

Dinner was served in what might have been the living room in an American home. They sat on the floor around a low, square table. Nori wasn't quite sure what to do with her legs at first. Put them under the table? Sit crossed-legged? She took her cue from Baba, who knelt gracefully on her thin cushion.

Only thing was, Nori wasn't used to sitting that way, and before long her knees started to ache and her legs cramped and she shifted around so much, she was sure they must have thought she was a total spaz.

Baba brought out a tray laden with several little plates and bowls with an assortment of food. The savory sweet smell of grilled chicken and onion kebabs made Nori's stomach rumble. There were also boiled soybeans, noodles with vegetables, and an egg-and-pork dish over rice.

It all looked awesome, but she hesitated. All she knew about meal etiquette was the basic stuff she'd read in her information packet. But what about when you're a guest in someone's home? Should you eat every scrap you're given? Leave a little on each plate? Eat slow? Fast? Belch? She watched Jiji, hoping to follow his lead, but he was more interested in talking than eating, and the way Baba kept jumping up to grab things from the kitchen, Nori was afraid they'd wear her out if the meal dragged on too long.

Finally, Nori decided to take the initiative and dig in. She reached for a plate and Baba quickly handed it to her.

"Thanks," Nori murmured.

She picked up her chopsticks. At least she knew how to use those. One less thing to feel stupid about. She picked up a bite.

"Nori-*chan*," Jiji said gently. "Before eating, it is polite to say, *'itadakemasu.'* It means 'I humbly receive.' You try it."

"Itadakemasu?"

"Very good." He gestured at the food. "Please. Begin."

As she had expected, everything was delicious. She ended up scarfing it all down, only to have Baba serve her seconds. By the time she finished with those, she was

stuffed. But they weren't through yet. Baba quickly cleared the plates and bowls and brought out little glass dishes filled with sliced strawberries in some sort of milky jelly.

Full to the point of aching, Nori leaned back against the wall, wishing she could unbutton her jeans. When Baba started clearing dishes, Nori struggled to sit up. "Please, let me help," she said.

"No, no, Nori-*chan*, you are guest."

"But—"

Baba shook her head emphatically. "Maybe you look at pictures," she said.

Before Nori could answer, Baba shuffled out of the room and returned with a large, leather-bound photo album. She gracefully knelt next to Nori, bowed, and held out the book with both hands.

Nori took the book and bent over the pages with interest, even though she didn't know any of the smiling kimono-clad people in the pictures. Or so she thought. When Baba turned to a section that looked like travel photos, Nori saw herself. At least it looked like her, but the clothes and hair were all wrong.

"Your mother," Jiji said.

No way. That grinning teenager in the faded T-shirt and torn jeans was her anal mom?

"She was so full of fire," he said. "You remind me a lot of her, Nori-*chan*."

She winced. Shows how much he knows. She and her mom were nothing alike.

Nori woke with a start. For a moment she couldn't recall where she was. She pushed back the overquilt and sat up, rubbing her eyes as she tried to focus on the room in the dim light. It came back to her with the lingering smells of last night's dinner and the old-house feel of Baba and Jiji's home.

The sound of dishes clinking drifted in from the kitchen. She squinted at her watch. It was barely five thirty. Who else was up? She stretched and padded to the window.

In the diffused early morning light, the yard looked like one of those softened picture postcards with its rock garden, meticulously pruned shrubs, and the graceful arch of the footbridge. And there was Jiji on the other side, bent over a patch of earth. Nori could hear the gentle *scritch, scritch, scritch* of his hand trowel as he worked the soil, and the low rumble of his humming.

He sat up to wipe his sleeve across his brow and looked toward the house. She pulled back from the window, not wanting to be caught spying.

In her *yukata* robe, Nori padded along to the bathroom. It wasn't until she saw the special plastic bathroom slippers neatly placed inside the door that she realized she had forgotten to put on her house slippers. She stepped quickly

inside and slid the door shut, wondering how much of a breach of etiquette it was to walk around in someone's house slipperless. She washed her face and brushed her teeth and pulled her hair into a ponytail before peeking out into the hallway, hoping to make it back to her room undetected.

"*Ohayo gozaimasu*, Nori-*chan*," Baba said.

Shakily, she returned Baba's smile, bowed and replied, "*Ohayo gozaimasu.*"

Baba beckoned for Nori to join her in the kitchen. Nori pulled on the front of the *yukata* as she went, curling her toes under the hem, hoping that Baba wouldn't notice her bare feet.

Baba glanced down briefly, but made no mention of it. She motioned for Nori to sit at the kitchen table. Unlike the low one where they ate dinner the night before, this table was Western-style with chairs and everything, but a little shorter than what Nori was used to.

She felt kind of weird about just sitting there, like she should be helping Baba instead of being served by her.

Baba seemed to sense Nori's discomfort because she paused, cupped Nori's face in both her hands, and said in her gentle, soft voice, "Very happy you are here." She pointed to Nori and then to herself. "Family. No worry."

Nori swallowed against a strange ache that settled in her throat. "No worry," she repeated. If only it were that easy.

Chapter Fourteen

THEY HAVE NO INTERNET HERE!
We're getting ready to go sightseeing this morning. I asked Jiji if I could use their computer to send Val a message before we went, and he looked at me as if I had sprouted two heads. They don't even own a computer. There goes my lifeline to the real world. I mean, I haven't been able to talk to Val about that whole Erik thing yet, and I won't get to tell her about Baba and Jiji for a whole week. I'm already having withdrawals.

Despite the early hour, the July sun beat down on them as they started off on their first day of sightseeing. It roasted them as they rode their bikes to the beginning of a sight-seeing trail. Jiji said they would walk from there.

Nori flapped her shirt and lifted her damp hair from her neck, wondering if it was as hot in Tokyo today. The rest of the group would be spending their first day with their host families. Would they be as miserable as she was?

Of course, her misery was compounded by the uncom-fortable weight settling on her chest the moment she thought about Tokyo. The events of that last night kept replaying in her mind like a bad sitcom. How could she have been such an idiot?

Baba touched her arm. "Do you feel well?"

"Oh. Yes. I'm fine."

Jiji gestured for her to quicken the pace. "There is much to see before the rains begin," he said.

Nori squinted at the sky. Not a cloud to be seen, but an approaching thunderstorm could account for the extra humidity. She fell into step beside him and Baba. The trail ran alongside a stone-lined canal, thankfully shaded under a canopy of ginkgo, maple, and cherry trees.

"This is called the Path of Philosophy," Jiji said.

Baba added, "It is very beautiful in cherry blossom sea-son."

"It's beautiful now," Nori replied.

Jiji nodded approvingly. "That it is. It's a fine thing to

appreciate simple beauty, Nori-*chan*. I think you will like *Ginkaku-ji*."

"What's that?"

"The Temple of the Silver Pavilion."

"Oh, yes!" Nori brightened. "I read about that one. It's not really silver, right?"

"See for yourself." He pointed to the temple compound just ahead.

When they entered the gate, Nori stopped dead in her tracks. The temple was perfect, like an ancient painting. It was actually brown instead of silver, with whitewashed panels and windows. It had two levels, each graced with upturned gables.

"This is it," she breathed.

Jiji raised his brows. "This is what?"

"How I saw it in my mind."

He nodded. "I felt the same way the first time I came here. This place was designed by the eighth Ashikaga Shogun to reflect the beauty of refined simplicity," Jiji said. "Some say he intended for it to be silver, but either he ran out of money or simply never got around to it."

"I like it the way it is," Nori said.

"Yes," Jiji agreed. "Some of the loveliest things in this life are gilded on the inside." He took Baba's hand and raised it to his lips. They smiled at each other in such a way that made Nori feel as if she were intruding. When she was old, she wanted someone to smile at her like that. But if her

parents couldn't find it, what made her think she could?

"Come," Baba said, blushing like a young bride. "You must see the gardens."

Baba and Jiji held hands as they followed a sand-covered path through Japanese pines and maples, raked rocks, and stone lanterns. Eventually, they came to the huge reflecting pond in front of the temple.

"Wow." Nori's voice was soft with wonder. "It's like a huge liquid mirror."

"Yes, that's exactly what it is," Jiji said. "See how the water reveals the beauty of the temple. A Zen master once wrote that a mirror has no ego, no self-consciousness. What it sees, it reflects, as simple as that."

Baba gazed out over the pond and said haltingly, "Old proverb say, 'As sword is soul of samurai, so is mirror soul of woman.' It mean mirror show woman's true heart. Look in the water, Nori-*chan*. If mirror is bright and clear, it mean your heart is pure and good."

Nori bent over the railing but couldn't bring herself to look at her reflection. She was afraid of what she might see.

Baba and Jiji stood in silence for a few minutes before Jiji laid a gentle hand on her shoulder. "Come," he said. "There is much more to do."

Nori followed them from the temple grounds. They continued along the path, visiting so many temples and shrines that everything began to blend together. When Baba suggested they stop for lunch, Nori was amazed that the morning had passed so quickly.

Jiji bought some *o-bento* lunch boxes and wheat tea from a convenience store while Baba and Nori spread a plastic mat in the shade. When he returned, they removed their shoes and sat on the mat to eat their lunch.

Nori fumbled with chopsticks, trying to eat the cold sesame noodles. They were a lot harder to pick up than the hot, sticky kind. Baba caught her eye and motioned for Nori to hold the container close and use the chopsticks to push the noodles into her mouth. It wasn't the most graceful way of eating, but it was a heck of a lot easier.

"How have you enjoyed Japan so far?" Jiji asked as they finished their meal.

Nori hesitated. "Uh, it's been very interesting."

"Your mother tells us you are studying about ecology."

"Yes. One of my classes is examining the Kyoto Accord, as a matter of fact."

"Ah." He nodded approvingly. "Perhaps soon we will have another crusader on our hands."

"Crusader?"

Jiji leaned back on his elbows, stretching his legs out in front of him. "Absolutely. Your mother and father were quite the activists in college. They met at a sit-in. Protesting apartheid, I believe."

Nori shook her head. No way. Her parents were way too

uptight about climbing the ladder to kick out the rungs along the way.

"Oh, yes," Jiji insisted. "They staged boycotts and rallies protesting everything from animal testing to sweatshop labor. Your father was even arrested once, as I recall."

Nori choked on her tea. She coughed and sputtered and Baba patted her on the back. "Arrested? *My* dad? What happened?"

Jiji chuckled. "Your mother was so proud of him, you'd have thought he won the Nobel Peace Prize. She boasted how he chained himself to a hundred-year-old oak tree to prevent the construction of a parking structure. You see, the preservationist instinct is a family trait."

The amusement of imagining her suit-and-tie dad chained to a tree like some psychedelic flower child was quickly eclipsed by an overwhelming mixture of anger and sorrow. So he'd go so far as to get himself arrested to save a bunch of acorns, but he would let his family fall apart. Some preservationist. And where was her mom's activist spirit now? Why wasn't she fighting to keep her marriage together? Nori closed the lid on her *o-bento* and stood. "I think I'd like to walk along the river for a bit," she said. "Do you mind?"

Baba and Jiji exchanged a look, but Baba said, "You go. We wait here."

Nori walked along the stone wall of the canal, kicking bits of twigs and pebbles into the water. She couldn't define the hurt and anger surging through her. Almost like her parents had betrayed her. Again. Hadn't she tried to be everything they wanted? Would she ever be smart enough, pretty enough, social enough, American enough, or Japanese enough to satisfy them? To make them want to be a family? To fight for it like they fought for other causes when they were young?

What was she going to do? What could she do? She'd never felt so helpless in her life.

Nori returned to continue the tour of the Path of Philosophy with Baba and Jiji, but her heart just wasn't in it. Even when they came upon the Chion-in Temple.

"You may recognize this place," Jiji said. "Have you seen *The Last Samurai*?"

"Lots of times," Nori said. "It's one of my dad's favorite movies." She wondered if she would ever watch it with him again.

"Ah, yes," Jiji continued. "Well, this is where they filmed several scenes."

Nori's eyes widened. She could see it now. The guards would have been standing right there at the base of the stairs, next to the *torii* gate. The film must have been doctored a little, because several of the surroundings were different, but this was the place, all right. Dad would just die if he knew she was here. She frowned. Before, she would have been excited to tell him. He would have made her describe

every detail. Would he even care now that he was leaving her behind?

"Is there something wrong?" Jiji asked.

"No," Nori said, turning away from the temple. "Just not a big fan of the film."

"Ah, I understand."

No, he didn't. But Nori kept that thought to herself.

The rains Jiji had predicted arrived by late afternoon. Baba produced two folding umbrellas from her bag. She and Jiji shared one, riding their bikes close together. Nori watched them all the way home, marveling at how they could still be so in love when they were so old.

It poured most of the evening. Nori watched the water splash down the chain-and-cup drain spout near her window and run in miniature rivers through Jiji's garden and into the koi pond.

The good thing about the rain was that it made everything smell all earthy and fresh. The bad thing was that it made the air unbearably sticky so that the moisture clung to your skin like cheap makeup.

Nori had always liked rainy days at home. She loved to listen to the sound of the water on the roof. Loved the security of being indoors, safe and dry, while the storm blew outside. But tonight the rain only made her feel hollow.

She rested her chin on the windowsill. Melancholy washed over her like the water in the spout.

This visit with Baba and Jiji signaled the beginning of the end. When she returned to Tokyo, there would only two weeks left in the term. Fourteen days until she had to go home. Three hundred thirty-six hours to try to salvage what she could of her S.A.S.S. experience and to clear the air with Erik and Atsushi. After that, she'd have no choice but to face her parents' separation.

She turned away from the window and flopped down onto her futon. No. She wasn't going to think about it anymore. Nothing she could do would change what was happening. She had put it out of her mind for four weeks; she could do it for three more. Didn't she have enough to worry about with school and Erik and her presentation and everything?

Jiji tapped on the door frame. "May I come in?"

Nori pushed herself up and sat cross-legged on the futon. "Sure," she said.

He stepped just inside and bowed. "Are you certain you would not like something to eat? Your aunt Rika—"

"Baba?"

"Yes. Baba fears you will not have the energy to visit Gion tomorrow."

Nori pushed a strand of hair from her face. "Gion? As in the Geisha district?"

"We were thinking of the teahouses. Baba has a friend who is an owner and would like for you to experience a traditional Japanese tea ceremony."

"Sweet."

"Actually, the tea can be quite bitter."

Nori laughed, mood lightening. "No, sweet means like 'cool.' 'Good.'"

"Very," he said. "Shall I report that you will eat a big breakfast in the morning?"

She gave him half a smile. "Sure. Thanks."

Jiji turned to leave, but paused at the door. "I also enjoy watching the rain," he said, gesturing to the open window with his chin. "It brings with it such promise." He bowed again. "*Oyasuminasai.*"

"Good night," she answered.

She lay in the dark and listened to the hushed shuffle of his footsteps, to the soft murmuring of Baba and Jiji's voices from down the hall, to the rain. Promise, Jiji had said. Of what? she wondered.

Chapter Fifteen

Entering the old quarter of Gion was like stepping back into another time.

"Why do I feel like I should whisper?" Nori asked in a hushed voice.

Baba smiled. "You sense dignity in this place."

She was right. There was an aura about the Gion district that spoke of refinement and modesty—not at all what Nori had expected. She'd imagined groups of geisha in colorful kimono mincing down crowded streets, giggling behind their hands as they greeted potential clients. Wasn't that how movies always portrayed them?

But here, now, such an image couldn't exist. Everything about Gion spoke of privacy, of respect. Teahouses, craft shops, and residences alike were protected from the view of strangers by bamboo blinds and rust-colored lattices. As they walked along cobbled streets, Nori caught a glimpse now and then of rice-paper shoji doors and tatami interiors, but only a glimpse.

Occasionally the strains of a beautifully sad melody would drift through a reed screen, just enough to make her want to hear more.

Baba nudged her and pointed to a particularly beautiful building across the street. "Here is most famous *ochaya*," she said.

"*Ochaya?* Is that a teahouse?"

"Different than teahouse," Baba said. "*Ochaya* is special place where geisha perform dance and music."

"And this one?" Nori shaded her eyes and looked across the street at the building's red walls. "Why is it so famous?"

"You know the story of the forty-seven samurai?" Jiji asked.

"Yeah. I mean, I've heard of it. They were the ones who killed the guy who dishonored their master, right?"

Jiji chuckled. "Yes, put very simply, you are correct. The Ichiriki *Ochaya* is where they hid while they were plotting their revenge."

"Ah." Nori looked again at the building, trying to imagine such drama taking place behind that dignified exterior. "Can we go see?"

"Oh, no. One must establish a relationship over many years before one is allowed to enter an *ochaya*."

"You're kidding. How do they stay in business?"

"Reputation is a very valuable commodity," Jiji said.

Nori couldn't shake the pinch in her chest. What kind of reputation did she have back in Tokyo? "Um, those samurai," she said, "didn't they end up killing themselves?"

Jiji nodded. "They were prepared to die in the name of honor." He glanced at his watch. "And now we must hurry. We are scheduled to participate in the tea ceremony in ten minutes."

Entering the teahouse felt very much like entering someone's home. The hostess, dressed in a peach-and-tan silk kimono, met them at the door and offered them clean slippers as they took off their shoes. She bowed deeply and said something to Jiji in a voice so soft that Nori could hardly hear.

"She welcomes us," Baba whispered, and motioned for Nori to follow the hostess as she led them through the house.

They walked right on out the back door, into a garden nearly as beautiful as Jiji's. Another little house stood near the rear of the yard.

"The teahouse," said Baba.

Near the door sat a stone basin with a bamboo ladle resting on its rim. Jiji stepped up to the basin. With his right

hand, he took the ladle and scooped up some water, which he poured over his left. He then transferred the ladle to his left hand and repeated the washing ritual to cleanse the right. Scooping again, he poured water into one cupped hand, sipped, and then spat onto the rocks at the side of the basin.

"To purify hands and mouth," Baba explained. She and Nori took their turns at the stone basin before the hostess showed them into the teahouse.

The doorway was really low, and even Baba had to duck to go under it. "This shows that all men are equal despite status or social position," Jiji explained.

The room that they came into was actually very plain. The only decoration was a scroll hanging in a small alcove, accompanied by a simple flower arrangement.

"This scroll painting is called *bokuseki*," Jiji whispered. "It means 'ink traces.' The kanji tells of a Buddhist scripture. We are to examine the scroll and compliment the hostess on her choice."

Nori swallowed. She didn't want to examine the scroll. The *bokuseki* looked too much like Amberly's calligraphy. The calligraphy that she had ruined because she was too caught up in her own drama to be aware of what was going on around her. She hung back, grateful for once for the language barrier, so she wouldn't be expected to say anything.

After they were seated on flat floor cushions near a low

table, polite greetings were exchanged, and a bowl of small, square sweets was passed around. Then the hostess began to prepare the tea.

Each movement was a carefully choreographed dance of the hands. Holding back her kimono sleeve, the hostess ladled hot water into the tea bowl. She rinsed the bamboo whisk, emptied the bowl, and dried it with a white linen cloth before scooping in the tea—all in smooth, graceful rhythm.

She poured in hot water and stirred the tea gently with the bamboo whisk. When the tea was ready, she picked up the bowl with both hands, bowed, and presented it to Jiji.

Jiji took the tea bowl and turned it around in his hand.

"He must not drink from front of bowl," Baba whispered. Nori was about to ask her why, but when Jiji had sipped from the bowl, he passed it on to his wife.

Baba also turned the bowl in her hands before she sipped. With all that turning, Nori wondered how they knew where the front of the bowl was. When Baba passed the bowl to her, Nori shrugged and followed what she had seen Baba and Jiji do. It seemed to please the hostess, so she must have done it right.

She took a sip. Aaagh! The tea was way too strong. And a little on the bitter side, just like Jiji had said. Nori fought to keep her face straight as she passed the bowl back to the hostess. "*Arigato,*" she managed.

Luckily, the strong ceremonial tea was followed by a

weaker tea to "cleanse the spirit before reentering the world," as Jiji said. Nori was just happy to get the taste of the strong tea out of her mouth.

Leaving the teahouse did feel like returning to another, harsher world. They said good-bye to the hostess and rode their bikes home in companionable silence. Nori's mind ran through the events of the day. Her thoughts kept coming back to the samurai, who were willing to die for the sake of honor, and the *ochaya*, businesses that were run on the strength of their reputation. This was her heritage. Her people. So why did she feel so small and weak? So far removed from it?

"Nori-*chan*?" Baba tapped on the door frame. "Mother is on telephone."

"My mom?" She pushed to her feet and followed Baba to the kitchen, worry gnawing at her gut. What's happened now?

Jiji sat at the kitchen table, receiver to his ear. "...not enough time with her. We'd love to have more." He looked up as Nori walked into the room. "Ah, here she is. I'll let you two talk. Take care, Mari-*chan*." He handed the phone to Nori and rose to leave.

Nori clutched his arm. "No. You can stay." She didn't want to be alone, in case...She raised the phone to her ear. "Hello?"

"Nori! Sweetheart. How are you?"

"I'm good. How is everything at home?"

"Fine, fine. So tell me about your visit with Uncle Kentaro and Aunt Rika. Aren't they delightful?"

Nori glanced at Jiji shyly. "Yeah, I really like them."

"You see? I told you you would. What have you three been up to?"

Nori gave her a play-by-play of the past two days.

"Sounds wonderful. I'm so pleased you had the chance to do this."

"So am I," Nori said. She wound the cord around her fingers. "So...is Dad there? Can I say hi to him?"

Silence.

"Mom?"

"Oh. Yes. I'm sorry, dear. Your father is...not around at the moment."

"When will he be back?"

"Oh, dear. I've got to run, sweetheart. I just noticed the time."

"Mom! Wait. Why did you call?"

Static crackled in Nori's ear for a moment before her mom's voice said softly, "I just needed to hear your voice."

Nori's throat tightened. "It's good to hear yours, too."

She hung up and looked at the phone for a long time before Jiji broke the silence.

"I think perhaps we are in need of a fun day tomorrow, what do you think?"

Nori gave him a trembling smile. "I think you're right."

• • •

Though sunlight already streamed through her window, the house was oddly silent when Nori woke. She sat up and squinted at her watch. Nearly seven o'clock. At this time of morning, Baba should be in her kitchen and Jiji in his garden. What was up?

She pulled on her *yukata*, crammed her feet into her slippers, and hurried down the hall to where Baba and Jiji's door stood partially open. The shades were drawn. She peered into the shadows to see Baba sitting up in her futon, Jiji pressing a teacup to her lips.

"Is everything okay?" Nori blurted.

Baba pushed the cup away. "*Daijobu*. I am fine."

"She felt faint."

"Pah! It was nothing. Just heat."

Jiji gave her a stern look. "You need to rest."

She moved to get up. "We promise Nori-*chan* fun day."

"Um, about that," Nori said. "I…uh…I have a lot of homework I need to get done. Would you mind if we take the day off today? It would really help me."

Jiji mouthed a thank-you and pressed Baba back down to her pillows. Under protest, Baba agreed to rest. Jiji calmly returned to his garden, but not before Nori noticed the muscle working in the corner of his jaw. He was more concerned than he was letting on.

Nori returned to her room and dressed slowly. She pulled out her books and stared at them for a long time. The end of the term was just over two weeks away, and she wasn't even close to being done with her presentation for the Global Outreach Summit. Her outline for a carbon emissions platform wasn't nearly completed. She needed to work on it, but she couldn't concentrate.

With a deep sigh, she looked out the window to see Jiji squatting near one of the bonsai trees, pruning shears in hand. He trimmed each branch with quick, deliberate movements. If she went out to watch, would he welcome the company or resent the intrusion?

Nori decided to take a chance that it would be the former. She peeked in on Baba, who was softly snoring, and tiptoed to the door to put on her shoes.

Jiji greeted Nori with a smile as she came around the corner of the house. "You have completed your homework already?"

She dug her hands into her pockets. "Not yet. I needed a break."

"I see." He clipped another small twig from the largest tree.

"This is really amazing," Nori said. "How long have you been working on it?"

He stole a glance at the house. "Years," he said.

"Was it hard to shape it?"

"Oh, I don't know." He took a wrinkled handkerchief from his pants pocket, removed his worn straw hat, and mopped his brow. "I wouldn't say it was hard. Not easy, but not

especially difficult. Each twist of the trunk, each sweeping branch is an opportunity to learn something new."

Jiji turned the ceramic planter to examine the tree from another angle.

"A beautiful bonsai requires daily care and a careful balance of what we call that *shin-zen-bi.*" He snipped a little nodule. "That's truth, essence, and beauty. The three are intertwined."

Another quick snip, and Jiji moved the container back to its original position. "Funny thing," he murmured. "Sometimes you set out to shape the bonsai and find in the end that the bonsai shapes you."

This time Nori looked to the house. Something told her that Jiji was not talking about trees.

The next day was not much cooler, but Baba refused to stay inside. "We must visit Nijo Castle," she said stubbornly.

"But…" Nori tried to keep her voice steady. She couldn't bear it if Baba got sick because she felt she had to take her sightseeing. "Are you sure you should?"

Baba waved her hand dismissively and gave Nori a wry smile. "Ach. Not ill. But maybe not so young, *ne*?" She tapped her head. "Many years, many memory." Then she touched a finger to Nori's forehead. "Much room for memory. Now we make another."

"Will you promise to sit whenever possible?" Jiji asked.

"No!" She marched out the door, Jiji trailing after her.

Nori hid a smile. No wonder the bonsai shaped him.

Jiji agreed to let Baba go—as if he had a choice—on the condition that they take a taxi instead of the bikes. Baba reluctantly agreed. It was only the second cab ride Nori had taken in Japan. She did not want to remember the first.

Baba was eager to show Nori every aspect of the Nijo Castle. She took her by the hand and led her from place to place, watching Nori's face closely as she asked, "You like?"

Of course Nori liked it. How could she not? From the moment they passed over the huge moat and entered the castle entrance, she felt the energy of the place. When they looked at the displays of samurai costumes, she could imagine fierce warriors inside them. Walking through the eleborate *Kara-mon* Chinese gate, she wondered if those warriors appreciated the stunning beauty of the painted cranes, flowers, tigers, and lions that decorated its panels. Did they sit in the palace garden and find serenity?

In the shogun's residence, she imagined them boldly standing guard or furtively slipping into the hidden rooms to keep an eye on potential enemies through watching holes concealed in elaborate paintings and carvings.

But her favorite part had to be the nightingale floors.

"These were a foolproof security system," Jiji said as they walked down the corridor, the floors squeaking beneath their stocking feet. Each step brought a chorus of chirps that

sounded like birds singing. "Special springs were built underneath the floorboards so that the slightest pressure would raise the alarm."

Nori bounced up and down on the balls of her feet to make them chirp even more. "This is sweet!"

Jiji leaned over to Baba and said in a loud whisper, "She means it's good."

"So these floors go around the whole building?"

"Yes, there was no way for an assassin to get in without crossing the floor and alerting the guards."

"That's pretty clever."

Nori would have liked to walk around the residence a few more times or explore the enchanting four-season garden, but she could tell Jiji was anxious to get Baba home. "Thank you," she said, kissing Baba's cheek. The skin felt fragile and dry. "It was fun to share this with you."

Baba's hand trembled as she raised it to her face. "Oh, Nori-*chan*. I will miss when you leave."

Nori drooped. Why did you have to remind me? She trailed behind Baba and Jiji as they left the palace, nightingales singing a sad farewell.

Chapter Sixteen

Nori lay on her futon staring at the ceiling. It wasn't fair. The time with Baba and Jiji had slipped by too fast.

Only one more day. And then?

Maybe she could pretend to be sick. Then they couldn't stick her on the train back to Tokyo. So what if she didn't finish the program? Maybe she could even refuse to go home. Then Mom and Dad would have to come here to get her. Together.

No, that was stupid.

She looked around her room, memorizing every detail.

The cloth binding on her tatami mats, the way the scroll on the wall curled in on the edges, the square wood panels on the walls. That way, if she needed an escape, she could come here in her mind.

Suddenly the room felt too small. She padded to the door and opened it quietly. The hallway still smelled of last night's curry. She held her breath and listened. The house was quiet. Silently, she tiptoed to the door, stepped into her shoes, and slipped outside.

On the porch, Nori closed her eyes. She breathed in the warm earth scent mingled with pine and the subtle sweetness from the daylilies near the stoop. Cicadas sang their night song, and a gentle breeze rustled the leaves on the trees and whispered in low tones through the bamboo chimes. It was heaven. And she was leaving.

Her shoulders sagged as she trudged along the path to the back garden to sit on the bench and mope.

Only someone had beaten her to it.

In the moonlight, Jiji sat straight-backed and still as a mountain, gazing out over the water of the pond. Nori shrank back into the shadows, holding her breath.

"Come sit with me, Nori-*chan*," he called softly.

She shook her head. "I'm sorry...I...I didn't mean to bother you."

"Companionship is never a bother."

Jiji's eyes never moved from the pond, but Nori had the

sensation he was watching her nonetheless. Quietly, she moved to the bench beside him.

They enjoyed the moonlight together in total silence. Nori contemplated its reflection on the water, thoughts tumbling through her head. She fingered the sash of her *yukata*, trying to formulate the words to ask Jiji for his advice.

He spoke first. "When I was a young boy, I went to live with family in Los Angeles. Like many Japanese, my parents had been fiercely loyal to the emperor, but they understood the value in adapting to a changing world." He closed his eyes and drew in a deep breath, as if conjuring old memories. "My mother's brother had moved to California many years after the war, and it was decided that I should spend my summers with him." He looked at her. "I did not wish to go, of course. I was a very dashing young man in those days, and my interest was in courting the beautiful girls of my country, not fighting the prejudice and language barriers of another. Yet, if nothing else, I was a dutiful son. I went each year, wearing one face in America and another when I returned home. At times I forgot which face was mine."

An ache settled in Nori's throat as she said, "So you know how I feel."

"Perhaps not completely."

It wasn't an invitation to dump. Nori knew it wasn't. But everything she had been locking away was like water in a dam, and all it took was that one little crack for it to break

through. "I don't know my face at all," she blurted. Jiji didn't say anything, so she continued. "I've spent so much time trying to be what everyone expects that I'm not sure who I am anymore."

He turned to her and nodded in understanding. "All significant battles are waged within the self, Nori-*chan*. You are fighting. That is what matters."

Her voice grew small. "But what if I'm fighting for the wrong side?"

His brows raised in question. She couldn't meet his eyes as she told him about the past several weeks in Tokyo. Of course, she left out the whole sneaking-out-to-a-nightclub thing. "I just don't know who I'm supposed to be anymore. My mom and dad never could agree on it, either. That was one of the things they fought about." A single tear rolled down her cheek, and she wiped it hastily away. She didn't want Jiji to think she was a crybaby. She was Japanese. She could be strong—she could *gambatte*. Even so, she couldn't stop the piteousness from creeping into her voice when she said, "If they break up, where does that leave me? Who am I then?"

"Nori-*chan*, there are things we can change and things we cannot change. A wise man knows the difference."

"Yeah, but—"

Jiji shook his head. "I think," he said as he stood, "perhaps we have time for one more site before you leave. There is something I would like you to see." He bowed. "Good night," he said, and he was gone.

Nori sat alone in the darkness for a while, feeling extremely stupid. *She pours her heart out, and that's all he can say? We should go to another tourist spot?* Maybe it was bad manners of her to have spoken about her parents like that. Not honorable or something. Somehow it seemed fitting that she would end her visit by doing something dumb.

Baba didn't accompany them on their outing the next morning, and Jiji would not tell her where they were going. It was all very mysterious.

Nori rode quietly beside him on her bicycle, still feeling rather foolish about her behavior the night before. Jiji seemed content to let the silence rest between them. He didn't speak until they reached their destination.

"The Ryoanji Temple," he said, climbing off his bike.

Nori parked her bike and followed him through the temple gate. The first thing she saw was a huge mirrored pond like the one at the Silver Pavilion. Her steps faltered. *Oh, great. He's going to make me look at myself in this one, too.*

But he strolled on by without so much as a glance.

Beyond it were the steps to the monks' and the abbot's quarters. They climbed wordlessly and walked through the buildings. Nori peeked in the altar room to see its painted dragons and stone grave tablets, but that wasn't what Jiji

was after either. To the rear of the monks' quarters was a tearoom. A low stone water basin stood beside the door. Jiji squatted down beside it.

We came to see a water basin?

"Look. There is an inscription on the bowl," he said, pointing out four kanji characters chiseled into the stone. "It says, 'I learn only to be contented.' It is a great Zen teaching."

Nori couldn't help but feel let down. That's what this trip was about? To tell her she should be content with the way things were? She managed to nod politely, not wanting to let her disappointment show.

"Now, then," Jiji said, standing to brush the wrinkles from his trousers, "let's go see what we came here for."

Oh. She was wrong. Again. She needed to learn not to second-guess Jiji.

Beyond the buildings they came upon a large rectangular arrangement of raked white pebbles surrounding a random assortment of stones. He stopped.

"Here we are."

"It's, uh, really something. What is it?"

"This," he said, "is a garden."

Garden? There were no plants, no flowers. Only the pebbles and the rocks and the clay wall surrounding them.

He sat on a worn wooden bench and removed his hat to mop the sweat from his head. "It is called a dry landscape garden," he said. "This particular garden is one of the most famous Zen gardens in all Japan."

Again with the Zen, huh? The only thing Nori knew about Zen was that it was all about clearing your mind… but once it was empty, what were you supposed to fill it up with again?

"The art of the garden," Jiji said in a low voice, "is to bring unity and harmony to the mind by its complex simplicity. Notice the empty spaces around the rocks. Very important for meditation."

He grew silent. Nori sat next to him and tried to figure out what it was he was looking at so intently.

After a long silence, he said, "Look at the garden and tell me what you see."

Oh, great. Now she got to reveal what an unenlightened idiot she was. "I see…rocks."

"How many?"

"Um…" She counted them quickly. "Fourteen."

"No. Count again."

She counted more carefully this time and still came up with fourteen.

"Actually, there are fifteen stones," Jiji said.

"Fifteen? No way." She moved to another spot in the gallery to count from another angle, but no matter where she stood, she could only count fourteen.

"The stones are arranged in such a way that only fourteen of the fifteen will ever be visible at one time," Jiji explained. "It is said that only those who have reached true Zen enlightenment can see the fifteenth stone."

She shook her head. "I don't get it."

"Nori-*chan*, many people spend their time looking for what cannot be seen instead of enjoying what lies in front of them. For those people, the fifteenth stone will always be hidden."

And as if that explained everything, he stood and sauntered from the gallery. Nori followed, feeling not the least bit more enlightened now than when she had come, and, in fact, a whole lot more confused.

Nori blinked back tears as the bullet train rolled out of the station. She pressed her face against the window and raised her hand in farewell as Baba and Jiji slipped away. She was leaving a part of herself on the platform with them, and in its place came a hollow, aching emptiness.

She took out her journal but could only stare at the pages, seeing on them the image of those fourteen stones. She heard Jiji's voice. "Some people spend their time looking for what cannot be seen." What did he mean?

Outside the window, she watched the countryside zip past. After a while, her eyes began to get heavy. She let them close. Gently, quietly, the thoughts in her head drifted away.

Enjoy what lies ahead of you, the wheels whispered over the track. Enjoy. Enjoy. What lies ahead of you. What lies ahead of you? A wise man knows. A wise man. A wise man.

She saw her parents' faces. Angry faces. Yelling. Her, trying to make it stop. Nori's eyes flew open. There are things I can change and things I cannot. Oh, Jiji, I get it now! You weren't talking about the things. You were talking about me.

Her parents fought. She could not change that. They chose to do the things they did. It was not her fault. It did not define her. A weight lifted from her shoulders.

But...

She was making choices, too. And only she could change the bad ones. Maybe she couldn't do anything about the mess her parents were making, but she could sure take care of her own.

"Enjoy what lies ahead of you," Jiji had said. But she couldn't. There would be no looking ahead until she cleaned up the past.

She could start with Amberly. Nori felt in her backpack for the comforting crinkle of paper surrounding the gift she'd bought. She'd seen a set of bamboo calligraphy brushes in a monk's booth just outside the temple and knew they'd be perfect for Amberly. It was a small thing, but she hoped the gift would serve as an apology. Maybe it wasn't too late to start over.

When the train rolled into Tokyo station, Nori was not surprised to find Amberly waiting to meet her on the platform. She waved through the window. By the time she made it to the vestibule, Amberly was in position, waiting to snap a picture as Nori stepped off the train.

"Thanks for coming," Nori said.

Amberly beamed. "So, how was it? Did you have fun? Was it weird being with your relatives? Did you see a lot of

neat places? I can't wait to hear all about it." She picked up Nori's backpack. "I took a lot of pictures of all the places I visited with my host family. You would not believe the iris garden at the Meiji Shrine."

Nori swallowed against a tight throat. She totally did not deserve such a warm welcome. "Thanks, Amberly," she said. "That sounds really nice. I'd love to see your pictures."

They stopped by Ms. Jameson's office first thing so that Nori could check in.

"I trust you had an enjoyable week?" Ms. Jameson asked.

"Yes, ma'am. Very much so."

"Good. Glad to have you back. Don't get too comfortable, though. We leave for the Fuji hike tomorrow afternoon."

Amberly set up the slide show on her computer while Nori unpacked her suitcase.

"Um, before we start," Nori said in a tight voice, "I have something I'd like to give you." She pulled out the package and handed it to Amberly.

"What is this?"

"Open it."

Amberly ripped back the paper and examined the brushes with a look of wonder on her face. "Real *sumi* brushes."

"Do you like them?"

"They're fabulous. Thank you, Nori. Wow. This is so unexpected."

Nori felt a little pang of guilt as she realized just how unexpected it must be. She hadn't done a single nice thing for Amberly the entire term. "I, uh…I wanted to apologize for how I acted before," she said.

"You didn't have to—"

"Yes, I did. I was horrible, and I'm sorry."

"You've been dealing with a lot." She lowered her voice. "I know how it is. My parents got divorced when I was twelve."

"Oh." Nori would never have guessed. Amberly seemed so sure of herself. So happy. "How did you know?"

"Things you've said. I recognize the confusion."

"Oh." Nori let that sink in. "Well, I am sorry."

"Forgotten." Amberly gave her a smile then set about arranging the brushes on her desk, completely wrapped up in the joy of the moment. Nori watched her, wishing she could be more like that. For all her quirks, Amberly was probably the most genuine person Nori had ever met.

She stood. Apologizing seemed so hard to do, but it sure felt good when you were done. "While you're getting that ready, would you mind if I pop over to Kiah's room for a minute? I have something I need to tell her."

Chapter Seventeen

Nori took extra care getting ready for breakfast. If she was going to have to confess to Erik, it wouldn't hurt to look her best while she did it. You never know. It might make him go a little easier on her.

Didn't do her much good, though. Erik never showed. She didn't see him or Atsushi at the cafeteria for lunch or dinner.

She asked Amberly about Atsushi as they gathered their things to go down to the bus.

"Oh, didn't I tell you? He had to go home for a couple of days. Some family thing."

"Nothing bad, I hope."

"Didn't sound like it, but he might not make it back by tonight."

Nori tried to swallow her disappointment. She had wanted to get his input before the talk with Erik.

As they were walking out to the bus, Amberly suddenly remembered that she'd left her camera hooked up to the computer. The two of them ran back up to the room to grab it, and when they got out to the buses, most everyone had already boarded.

Wada-*sensei* waved them toward the nearest bus. "Hurry up, girls," he called. "The mountain waits for no man—or woman."

"But I wanted to check and see which bus—"

"The time for checking is gone. Let's move it."

All the seats were taken except for the geek-seats directly behind the driver. Nori and Amberly slid into them, the doors closed with a hydraulic hiss, and they were off. As coolly as she could, Nori twisted around to see if Erik was on her bus. He was not.

"Don't look so disappointed, mate," said Kiah, who was sitting one row back on the opposite side of the aisle. "He's surely on the other bus."

Heat spread across Nori's cheeks. "Who?"

"Whoever you're searching for with that moon-dog look on your face."

Was it that obvious? "Oh, I was just seeing who's here."

Kiah chuckled. "Uh-huh."

It was good to laugh with her again. Even though Kiah had never held a grudge about the whole fish market thing, Nori felt better for having made the effort to apologize. "So," Nori asked her, "how did your home stay go?"

"Way to change the subject." Kiah grinned, winking one green eye. "But since you ask, it went well. I stayed with a very nice family."

Amberly leaned forward. "Oh, you were with Akina's family, right? She's in my Eastern philosophy class. What did you guys do?"

Nori lost track of the conversation. She was too busy fretting about how she was going to approach Erik when she finally saw him again. It was just as well he wasn't on the bus because Nori spent the entire ride trying to figure it out. No matter what scenario she envisioned, she couldn't come up with a way to tell him the truth without coming off like a total idiot. Probably because she had been a total idiot. Not much use in denying it.

"Look, there it is!" Amberly said, practically bouncing out of her seat.

Nori craned her neck to see out the opposite windows. Mount Fuji stood in the distance, like an upside-down ice-cream cone with the point bitten off. There was no draping of white at the top like on her postcards. Too late in the season, she figured.

As they drew closer, the summit became less visible until Nori could not see it at all. She stared out the window as the bus began its long climb, the evening sunlight casting long shadows across the mountain's winding road. On many stretches, bamboo and firs lined both sides, but on the outside turns, guardrails were all that stood between them and a steep drop down the side of the mountain.

"Look, we're getting higher!" Amberly said. "We're almost there!"

Almost there. The words churned in Nori's head.

After what seemed like miles of zigzag roads and hairpin turns, the bus pulled into a wide parking area. "This," Amberly announced, "must be the fifth station."

"The what?"

"The mountain is divided into ten stations from the bottom to the top. We can only drive up as far as the fifth station, so that's why we have to hike the rest of the way."

Nori nodded her understanding and swung her backpack over her shoulder. They climbed off the bus. The other bus hadn't arrived yet, Nori noted with some relief. As much as she wanted to see Erik, she still didn't know what she was going to say to him when she did.

Amberly tugged on her arm. "Come on. Let's go look at the shops while we're waiting."

The shops in question were a row of completely touristy storefronts lined up at one end of the parking lot. They weren't exactly what Nori had pictured when she thought of the stately mountain.

"Sad, isn't it." Wada-*sensei* stepped up beside them,

shaking his head. "So many people make it only as far as this point, and they think this is what Fuji is all about. They'll buy a souvenir so they can say they've been here, but, if you ask me, they haven't really seen it."

"Maybe," Amberly countered, "but I do want one of those walking sticks."

They wandered through the stores for a while, but Nori's heart really wasn't in it. She tapped Amberly on the shoulder. "I'll wait outside."

Still no sign of Erik's bus, so she paced the sidewalk behind the vendors' carts. Something cooking in one of them smelled really good—toasty and savory and just a little sweet. Nori's stomach rumbled. She watched a man in a white apron painting brown sauce over what looked like skewered golf balls. A little hand-lettered sign on the front of the cart read, DANGO, 300 YEN. Well, that didn't tell her much. For all she knew it was made out of fish guts. Didn't smell fishy, though.

She stepped up to the cart and held up one finger. The vendor took her yen and handed her three little roasted balls on a stick. She wandered over to a shadowed bench and sat, waiting for the *dango* to cool enough to eat.

She looked to the shop. Amberly was still in there, examining perfectly identical walking sticks, as if somehow she was going to be able to find one better than all the others.

Nori took a big bite from one of the balls. The sides gooshed outward and the whole thing came off the stick and into her mouth. Agh. No idea it was so big. And it seemed to be growing. Filling every crevice of her mouth. Like thick, sweet paste.

She stood, desperately looking for a water fountain so she could wash the gunk down.

What she saw was Erik stepping off the other bus.

He waved at her. She forced the best smile she could manage and returned the wave. Great. He was coming over. Nori's eyes darted left and right. What was with this place? No drinking fountains and no garbage cans. She tried in vain to swallow, but the *dango* wouldn't budge. Even worse, the sauce was making her salivate and there was like a gallon of spit in her mouth.

She hurried into one of the stores and hid behind a rotating rack of postcards until she could manage to choke it down.

"Getting some cards?"

Nori twisted around to find Wada-*sensei* looking down at her, brows raised. "Uh, yeah." She grabbed a few at random and stood.

"Think I'll get a couple, too. My wife still gets a thrill out of getting something postmarked from the top."

"The top?"

"Yes, from the post office on the rim. Isn't that what you're getting those for?"

"Oh. Yeah."

"Hey, where'd you get the *dango*? I love that stuff."

"Here, you can have it." She handed him the remaining two balls on the skewer. "What's it made of, anyway?"

"Pounded rice," he said, matter-of-factly.

Figures.

Nori paid for her cards and found Amberly. By the time she made it back outside, Erik was nowhere to be seen. Great. He probably thought she was a real flake, running off like that. Or he thought she was trying to avoid him. Either way, it wasn't good. She had to find him and explain.

Hustling Amberly over to the base of the trail, she searched for him, but there were only a handful of students there, and none of them was Erik. He must have gone ahead already.

Ms. Jameson glanced up from her clipboard. "You're late," she said. "You'll have to wait with the other stragglers to be assigned a group." A few minutes later she cleared her throat and said, "All right, people, listen up. This is the last time I am going to repeat these instructions. In order to reach the top of the mountain by sunrise, we will be hiking through the night. You will stay with your assigned group, and when we reach the eighth station, your group will check in with me again. Together. Until that time, you are responsible for each other. Do not leave your group. Do not step off the trail. Be courteous and careful."

With that, she divided the remaining students into groups of five and sent them off in waves. Nori balled her hands in frustration as she realized hers would be the last to leave. At this rate, she was never going to catch up to Erik.

"Come on, Nori!" Amberly called. "Let's take a picture of our group before we start."

Nori looked over to where Amberly stood, camera in hand. Right behind her, arms folded across her scrawny chest, stood Michiko, lips curled in a disdainful sneer.

Perfect.

By about the seventh station, Amberly's walking stick didn't look like such a dumb idea after all. In the beginning, the trail hadn't been too bad, but it got steeper and rougher the higher they climbed. The sun had long since set, and moonlight was not enough to illuminate the dips and bumps in the path. Nori could have used something to lean on.

There was no slowing down, either. A steady stream of hikers moved along the trail so everyone either had to keep up the pace or move out of the way.

Michiko tripped along in front of Nori, muttering to herself in Japanese. Nori half wished that she could understand what the grumbling was about. Not that it would help. An iceberg couldn't be colder than Michiko.

As fate would have it, while Nori was musing about Michiko's lack of social skills, Michiko slowed down, and Nori stepped right on her heel, squishing down the back of one of her Nikes.

"Watch where you step," Michiko snapped.

Nori bit her tongue. "Sorry," she muttered.

"You are a clumsy cow," Michiko proclaimed.

"And you're a...oh, forget it." She gritted her teeth. Being enlightened sure was hard.

"Look! Up there." Amberly pointed with her stick. "It must be the eighth station. We're almost there."

And about time, too.

They climbed toward a cluster of lights, the confusion of voices growing louder as they approached. When Nori could finally make out shapes in the shadows, her heart dropped. This was where they were supposed to be resting?

Hundreds of people milled about a couple of squat concrete buildings that looked more like bomb shelters than lodges. She'd hardly been expecting luxury, but come on.

"Don't worry," Wada-*sensei* said as he stepped up alongside them. "We're not staying there. We have reservations on terra firma."

"Very funny," Nori said.

"Terra Firma?" Amberly asked. "Where's that?"

Wada-*sensei* laughed. "Come on, I'll show you. We're gathering just up the rise there."

"Wait. I need to get my stick chopped."

Nori pressed her lips together. They'd had to stop and get the stick stamped, or chopped, as they called it, at all the other stations, which meant waiting in long lines and getting farther and farther behind on the trail.

Running a hand over his head, Wada-*sensei* said, "Well, okay. If you're quick about it. Tanaka, go with her. You have ten minutes."

"Arigato!" Amberly grabbed Nori's hand. "Come on!"

Nori spotted a booth just outside the first hut. "There," she said, pointing.

"No. Those are just ink stamps. I want mine burned."

They wove their way through the crowd until they smelled the tang of wood smoke. About a dozen people milled in front of a makeshift booth where a man sat, holding what looked like a miniature branding iron, the hot end glowing red in the darkness. One by one, with excruciating slowness, he stamped the sticks and collected the money.

As they neared the booth, they caught a whiff of another, less-pleasant smell mingling with the burned wood.

Nori cringed. Not more than ten feet away from the booth stood a rickety row of outhouses. Worse, one man was relieving himself right out in the open into a trough that ran alongside the latrines. "Oh, now that's just wrong," she said. "Let's go."

"But my stick."

"Can't you just get it ink-stamped this one time?"

"It would rub off."

Nori heaved a sigh and then immediately wished she hadn't—in the process, she'd taken in a deep breath of foul air. "Fine," she wheezed. "I'll wait for you over there." She pointed to a clearing a good distance away. Upwind from the latrines.

Good thing she'd listened when Amberly told her to bring an extra sweater. The night air was getting colder by the

minute. She hugged herself and waited, absently looking around the station. She blinked. Was that Atsushi coming around the corner?

"Atsushi!" Waving, she ran to him. "It's so good to see you!" She flung her arms around his neck. He stiffened and she let go. "I...uh...I missed you."

In that cute, dorky way of his, he cocked his head to the side and furrowed his brows. "So where's Sussmann? I thought you two would be together."

"Got it!" Amberly pranced up, waving her stick victoriously. When she saw Atsushi, she stopped and squealed like a little kid. "You're back!" She pushed past Nori to give him a hug. He didn't pull away from her, Nori noticed with a pang of—what? Jealousy?

"Where's your group?" Atsushi scanned the crowd.

"Everyone's meeting up on the ridge," Amberly said, slipping her arm through his. "You can walk with us."

He shot a look at Nori and disentangled his arm. "You go on," he said, stepping back. "I'll see you up there." Then, without a word of explanation, he disappeared into the blackness.

A weight settled in Nori's chest. What just happened?

Chapter Eighteen

When they reached the ridge, the groups had already gathered together into one huge cluster. Ms. Jameson stood before them with a clipboard in hand, conducting roll call.

"She called you already," Kiah whispered to Amberly. "You better talk to her after."

Nori leaned close. "What are we doing?"

"This is where we take a load off, mate."

"Shiota," Ms. Jameson called.

"Here." Atsushi's voice sounded close. Nori's stomach did a funny sort of flipping thing. Where was he? She searched for him in the shadows as roll call continued.

"Skinner."

"Here."

"Sussmann."

Nori froze. Right. And him, too. Where was he?

"Here."

"Tanaka."

"Here," Nori cried.

"Good evening," a deep voice rumbled in her ear.

"Erik." She turned to face him. Goodness! He was looking fine in his hiking shorts. This was going to be harder than she'd thought.

He frowned. "Where did you go? I thought I saw you near the shops."

"Oh, yeah. I was just...never mind." She touched his arm. "Erik, I need to talk to you." Eyeing the swarm of students around them, she added, "In private."

His frown slowly gave way to a knowing smile. He winked and grabbed her hand. "Come." He pulled her away from the group.

Darkness enveloped them. Even though they were probably not more than ten feet away from the others, Nori was suddenly very aware of the isolation. He turned to face her, so close that she could feel the heat of his body next to hers. Her heart danced like it was going to jump right out of her chest. She knew she had to tell him about the deception, but now, standing near him, touching him, she felt her resolve begin to crumble.

He cupped her chin in his hand and tilted her face up to his. Washed colorless in the moonlight, with his chiseled features and blond hair, he looked like a statue of some hot Norse god. She licked her lips. "Erik..."

"Shhh." His arm slithered around her waist and pulled her tight against him.

She tried to push back. "I need to tell you—"

"I know."

"But—"

"No words." He bent toward her, soft whiskers rubbing against her cheek. He smelled of sweat and shampoo. "Welcome back, my little geisha," he murmured.

"Hey. I'm not your—"

He smashed his lips against hers.

"No!" She pulled away. "Stop that. I'm not—"

"Hush. We will talk later."

He came at her again, but she turned her head, and his kiss landed on the side of her nose.

"You don't understand. I—"

Laughing, he pulled her into a hug. She pushed away.

"Erik, listen to me! I am trying to tell you something."

"And I'm trying to—"

"Shut up and listen! I haven't been completely honest with you, okay? I'm not from Tokyo, I'm from Ohio. You know...in America?"

"But..." The smile disappeared from his face. "You do not look American."

"Well, my family is originally from Japan. But I was born and raised in the U.S.A. I should have told you. I just—"

"You lied to me?"

Her face felt as if it might spontaneously combust. "Yes," she said in a small voice. "I...I just wanted you to like me."

"And you thought I would not if you were not Japanese?" He looked at her as if she were something gross he had just discovered on the bottom of his shoe. "You think I am so shallow?"

Ouch. It sounded bad when you put it that way. "I...I was wrong, Erik. I'm very sorry." Without thinking, she bowed to show her humility.

He snorted. "You do not have to act anymore," he said, lip curling in distaste. "I am no longer impressed."

She watched him go, the swagger in his step now infuriating instead of attractive. She tightened her jaw. What had she ever seen in him? He was a Neanderthal. A typical male-chauvinist, drink-swilling Neanderthal. But then what did that make her?

He wasn't the one who had lied.

Chapter Nineteen

Amberly had the good graces to leave Nori alone—at least until it was time to start hiking again.

"You doing okay?" she asked gingerly.

"Fine," Nori replied. If only she meant it. The whole thing with Erik had left her shell-shocked. But what did she expect? A relationship built on a lie is doomed from the start.

She tried to do the Zen thing and empty her mind. Didn't work. She had to think about *something*.

She chose to concentrate on the mountain and the climb. Focused in on the roughness of the path, the stones beneath her feet, the sharp scents of earth and dirt and the freshness

of early morning dew. She welcomed the burning sensation in her muscles, knowing that each step took her nearer to the top.

As the velvet blackness of the sky lightened to purple, the group neared the final leg of the hike.

"Hurry," Wada-*sensei* urged. "We don't have much time!"

The summit lay just above them, stark black against the predawn sky, distanced by the steepest and roughest portion of the trail yet. With a final burst of energy, Nori climbed, grasping the rough volcanic rocks with her hands to speed her progress. Sharp edges bit into her skin, but she didn't care; she'd blown everything else, but she was going to see the sun rise on Fuji.

Amberly struggled up the slope a few feet behind her, hampered by that stupid stick of hers. Nori hesitated for a moment. She looked up at the ridge then back down at Amberly then sighed heavily—not an easy thing to do in the thinning air.

"Here, give me the end," she said.

Amberly looked at her quizzically, sucking in shallow breaths.

Nori rolled her eyes. "The stick. Give me the end of your stick."

Using it as a tow rope, she hauled Amberly up behind her and struggled to the top. She could tell by the rosy glow above the rim that the sun was just about up. "Come on!"

Suddenly the slope leveled out and the summit lay right

ahead. They climbed the final steps to pass under a wooden *torii* gate and stood on the ridge, panting and hugging. It wasn't quite the solitary experience Nori had envisioned. Hundreds of others stood on the rim as well, panting, crying, a few of them looking bored. She could see some of her group nearby, laughing and giving high fives.

"We did it!" Amberly wheezed. She gave Nori a reproachful look. "You could have missed this."

Nori snorted. "Are you kidding? We had plenty of time. If I thought I was going to miss it, I'd have left you behind."

Before Amberly could say something that might lead to another mushy, girly bonding moment, Nori turned away. No. She would not have wanted to miss this.

From this height, she could see for miles in all directions as the sun gilded the mossy greens and browns of the Kanto Plain. No matter what had happened, no matter what went before, this was without a doubt worth it all. It was the most amazing thing Nori had ever seen. Even better than Shibuya at night.

Thinking of Shibuya—and Atsushi—brought with it a pang of regret that spoiled the euphoria Nori wanted to be feeling, so she filed it away for later. No more looking for things that were not there.

She wandered over to a rock and sat down, looking out over the valley. Towns and forests looked like toy layouts. Houses and farms like miniature pastoral scenes. She felt powerful sitting here with the world at her feet.

But also very small. Overwhelmed by the size of the mountain, by the vastness of the land and the sky.

Interesting how a change in vantage point could make such a difference in the way she saw things. She laughed to herself, imagining Jiji having some kind of Zen wisdom to share about that.

Then it happened. In the midst of all that chaos, Nori had an epiphany. She'd never had one of those before, but she'd read about them enough back home in lit class to know that's what it was. The revelation came to her so clearly she could almost touch it. Right then she knew she needed to change her presentation for the summit.

With no paper to write on, she dumped out her lunch, found a pen, and started to rewrite her speech on the back of the paper bag. It might not be a scholarship winner, but it wasn't about that anymore. Nori had come to Japan to get away from her life, but instead she felt like she had found it.

With less than two weeks left in the term, the casual atmosphere at school started to change. Tension mounted. Finals loomed. The summit presentations awaited completion. No one had time to hang out in the courtyard anymore, or to make late-night runs to Shibuya. Everyone pretty much kept to themselves. Nori was no exception. For three days before finals, she hardly slept. The upside was that she didn't have much time to worry about Erik or Atsushi or anything else for that matter. She spent all her conscious hours reading, reviewing, and running through flash cards and practice questions until she thought her brain would explode.

Finally, the dreaded day of reckoning arrived. Nori felt pretty good about ecology and culture. Econ was iffy. But she aced Japanese history. Who knew? The time with Baba and Jiji had connected her with the past—her past—in a way she never would have dreamed.

Even with finals behind her, though, she couldn't slow down. There was still the summit to get through. She shifted gears to hammer out her speech on the computer. Amberly, meanwhile, used her new brushes to finish her calligraphy. She was very secretive about it, though, and wouldn't let Nori see the completed project until her presentation.

On the morning of the summit, Amberly went to school early to set up. When Nori arrived, Amberly met her at the door. "Close your eyes," she said. She took Nori by the hand and led her through the hallways toward the auditorium. "Okay," she said, pulling to a stop. "You can look now."

Nori opened her eyes. "Oooh."

"Oooh, what? Do you like it?"

"Amberly, it's…it's absolutely stunning." She gaped at the main hallway, lined with about three dozen rice-paper banners featuring Amberly's kanji, paired with black-and-white photographs.

"It's called the Wall of Peace," Amberly said softly. "Is that lame?"

"Not even. It's awesome." Nori walked slowly down the

hall, examining each picture. She recognized some of the subjects; they were Global Outreach students. Many more were strangers. In all of them, Amberly had captured something in their faces, in their eyes. They came alive on the paper. "Where did you take these?"

"Around." Amberly smiled sheepishly. "In case you haven't noticed, I carry my camera everywhere."

Nori stopped dead in her tracks when she saw Michiko's face gazing out from one of the banners. The determined set of her chin was right on. Her eyes were focused on some unseen target. It was total Michiko.

"She represents 'challenge,'" Amberly said, tracing the kanji character with her finger. Nori opened her mouth to make a snide remark about just how much of a challenge Michiko was when Amberly added, "I admire how strong she is, how she deals with obstacles head-on. We need people like that to push us, you know?"

The five-minute warning bell sounded. Reluctantly, Nori followed Amberly into the auditorium. She wanted more time to wander through the banners and see who else Amberly had managed to capture on film. Was there a picture of her in there? What would her kanji say?

Kiah waved from the front of the room and motioned for them to come over, pointing to two vacant seats near hers and Kirsti's. "When're you up?" she asked as Nori sat next to her.

"Number ten this afternoon. You?"

"Fourth in line this morning. Look who's last before lunch." She pointed to the program. "Sussmann. Talk about spoiling your appetite."

Before Nori could respond, the lights in the auditorium dimmed, and Ms. Jameson took the podium. "All right, people. Settle down." She banged a gavel, the hollow wooden thunk echoing through the auditorium like a shot. The room fell silent. Satisfied, she settled narrow glasses on the end of her nose, cleared her throat, and read from her paper. "Whereas the Global Outreach program and Students Across the Seven Seas are dedicated to raising awareness of and taking action to improve conditions of international social, economic, ecological, and developmental progress, we hereby call to order this Global Outreach Summit and charge each participant with the responsibility to promote international understanding and goodwill. May we each learn and use our knowledge to make a difference in the world."

Nori tried to listen to the speeches and proposals presented, she really did. But she couldn't concentrate on any of them. She kept running her own over and over in her head, hoping that she hadn't made a mistake in abandoning her presentation on emissions exchange. Would they understand what she was trying to say?

Not that anyone was really paying attention to all the

presentations anyway. They were only supposed to be five minutes each, but five minutes times about eighty presentations was a lot to sit through.

By the time Erik's turn finally came, it looked like half the audience was asleep and the other half was off in a world of their own.

He stepped up the microphone and stood silent. For a long time. A buzz rose from the delegation. He forgot his speech. He's not prepared. He's got stage fright. Finally, when he had everyone's attention, he gripped the podium with both hands and with a confident voice declared, "No more waiting."

Some students laughed. Others clapped or whistled.

"The greenhouse effect can be reversed," he continued. "Reforestation is the answer." Using PowerPoint charts and graphs, he addressed the cost and difficulty of reforestation in industrialized nations where carbon sinks were sorely needed, and presented what sounded like pretty good solutions: greening up highways, using hedges as fencing, introducing hearty vines to drought-stricken areas.

Nori had to give him credit. He'd taken what Atsushi had said to heart, even bashing some of his earlier hypothesis as impractical.

"The answer is action," he concluded, "and the time is now."

Spontaneous applause erupted as he bowed curtly and sat down.

When the meeting was adjourned and the lights came up, Nori stood and moved toward the stage.

Kiah raised her brows. "Where you going?"

"To congratulate him."

"You gotta be kidding. After the way he treated you? Have some pride, girl."

"He did a good job."

"He's a jerk," Kiah said.

Nori set her jaw. Anyone who could express himself the way Erik just did couldn't be all bad. He had given one seriously fabulous presentation. She felt he deserved a word of congratulations, that's all.

She worked her way through the swarm of people standing in the aisle and stood patiently behind Erik as he received his kudos from the faculty. Kikuchi-*san* noticed her and smiled.

"*Konnichiwa*, Nori," she said.

Stiffening, Erik turned to face her, blue eyes like ice. Nori suppressed a shiver and extended her hand.

"Nice job," she squeaked.

Erik made no attempt to shake her hand, but let it dangle in the air between them. She stuffed it into her pocket.

"Well, just wanted to tell you I thought it was good." Good? How lame could she be?

He sniffed. Actually sniffed his disdain like some low-budget actor in a B movie and turned away without a word.

Kiah stepped up beside Nori. "Someone needs to tell that

jackaroo to get over himself." She took a step toward him. "I'll give 'im a gobful."

"No." Nori laid a hand on her arm. "It's okay. It's my fault."

She snorted. "Don't care whose fault it is. No one deserves to be treated like less than they are."

Nori swallowed. When you're right, you're right. Only she wasn't thinking about herself, she was thinking about Atsushi. He definitely deserved an apology for the way she had treated him. If only she knew how to go about it.

Nori's presentation was scheduled for that afternoon. She gripped her papers in both hands, palms sweating. The walk to the microphone took forever. Behind the podium, she shifted her weight from one foot to the other, swallowing against a dry throat. When she finally spoke, her voice sounded distant, as if the words were coming out of someone else's mouth.

"The view from the fifth station is very nice," she began. "You can see the valley below, the road winding like a ribbon to the mountain. A lot of people are happy with this view. They come, they see, and they think they know what the world looks like from Fuji. But I know better."

She went on to explain how from each higher station on the climb up the mountain, the view was successively broader. From the top, the things one could see were much different from what was viewed from the fifth station.

"Knowledge shifts our perspective as surely as a climb up

the mountain," she concluded. "Once we have observed and studied and climbed to the highest vantage point, we can shift our internal perspective. And then we have the responsibility to reach out and help those who can't yet see."

She stepped back.

Silence.

Nori smiled shakily and picked up her papers once again, straightening them in her hands. "Um... Thank you," she said into the microphone.

Someone in the back started to applaud, slowly at first then in quicker cadence, joined by a few more until everyone in the auditorium was clapping.

Nori's knees went weak with relief. She staggered from the stage. Yes. It was over.

Or... No. It had just begun. Because although she had been talking globally, Nori felt the effects of that internal perspective shift on a personal level. It was time for her to take the responsibility seriously.

Chapter Twenty

The rest of the summit raced by. In the end, she had no idea what any of the other presentations even were. It came as no surprise when Erik was announced as the Global Outreach scholarship winner. Despite everything that had passed between them, Nori was happy for him. Not that she was going to congratulate him. She wasn't quite enlightened enough to try that again.

Back in the hall, she had to wait in line to get a peek at Amberly's banners. Everyone was pointing, commenting, nodding like they were in some big New York gallery. Nori was walking along, peering over shoulders and heads, when she saw it. Her face on one of the banners. She was gazing off in the distance, a faraway look in her eyes.

"The kanji says 'vision,'" Amberly whispered.

Nori could only nod. She hoped her vision would improve as she looked ahead, instead of—

A sharp crack from behind them startled her. Nori swung around to see Michiko standing with fists at her sides while a stunned Erik held one hand to his cheek.

"I am not your anything," Michiko spat. "Do you even know what geisha are? They are artists, not prostitutes! Artists who would never waste their time on a pig like you!" She turned on her heel and stomped away.

"Well, that was long overdue," Kiah said.

"I think he just got a new perspective," Amberly added with a smile. "The conference couldn't have ended better."

Nori laughed. Wasn't that the truth! Except, for her, the conference hadn't quite ended. There was still one thing she had left to do.

Nori followed Atsushi from the school grounds but didn't catch up to him until he paused on the train platform. She walked up behind him and tapped his shoulder.

"Excuse me," she said. "Could you help me?"

He turned around, the same unreadable expression on his face as she'd seen at Mount Fuji.

It was almost enough to make Nori lose her nerve. "I...uh...I'm lost."

His eyes softened, and his mouth twitched. He tightened his lips against a smile. Well, that was a good sign, right? Cocking his head, he said, "Oh, you are, are you?"

"'Fraid so. See, I had this great friend and I took advantage of him, and I need to find a way to say I'm sorry."

He furrowed his brows. "Wow. That's serious."

"Very. What do you think I should do about it?"

"Well, you could take this friend to dinner. You know, to show you're sincere and all."

Nori smiled. "You're on."

Late that evening, Nori was still smiling. She must have looked totally goofy, but she didn't care. She smiled as she brushed her teeth, smiled as she got ready for bed. Smiled as she IM'd Val from Japan for the last time.

> **Valerivalera:** So where did U go?
>
> **Revengelobster:** Don't remember the name of the place. Had great Katsudon, though.
>
> **Valerivalera:** Whatever. Want to hear about BB.
>
> **Revengelobster:** Funny thing, that.
>
> **Valerivalera:** What?
>
> **Revengelobster:** Don't feel compelled to talk about it.
>
> **Valerivalera:** Dish it, girl!
>
> **Revengelobster:** Let's just say there was more 2 him than 1st imagined.

Nori closed her eyes, remembering. Oh, there was more.

It had really been weird at first. Awkward. Nori wasn't quite sure what she should say. Sorry for using you to get to another guy? Sorry for taking you for granted? Sorry for …well, there were just too many things. And Atsushi didn't seem to know what to say to her, either. Likely the same thoughts were running through his mind. She'd been a first-class witch, and they both knew it.

But once they got started, they talked and laughed non-stop until the restaurant closed and the manager had to ask them to leave. Everything else just sort of melted away. Nori didn't even give Erik or her parents' separation or the results of the scholarship awards a second thought the whole evening.

Something between her and Atsushi changed—something that Nori couldn't quite define.

Maybe it was the jolt she felt when Atsushi took her hand as they walked back to the train. That was something she definitely hadn't expected—the hand-holding or the jolt. She was so surprised that it actually took her a moment to catch her breath. By then her senses were on high alert. She was hyperaware of everything: the pressure of his fingers, the warmth of his hand, the way it was both soft and rough at the same time.

Maybe it was the way he turned to her when they had reached her dorm-room door and got all shy on her again.

He actually blushed as he bowed and gave her his *meishi* address card. His voice got all soft and hoarse when he asked her if she would write to him.

But oh, yes, for sure it was what happened next.

"I'll only write if you promise to write back," she said.

He readily agreed to her terms. And as she looked into his obsidian eyes, the jolt she felt earlier was totally eclipsed by a melt-on-the-floor bolt of lightning.

Oh. My.

Now why hadn't she picked up on that before?

And then… well, then came the clincher.

He stepped closer. Bent toward her. Brushed his lips against hers. That's all it was. A soft, gentle kiss. But, oh! When he pulled away, Nori could hardly even breathe.

"Good night," he said.

Absolutely. That it was.

Valerivalera: HELLOOOO? Earth to Nori. U still there?

Revengelobster: Sorry. Um, got sidetracked.

Valerivalera: So, U R not going to tell me about BB?

Revengelobster: 'Fraid not.

Valerivalera: What about HH?

Revengelobster: Nothing to tell.

Valerivalera: Hope U know U will not get away with this stonewalling when U get home. Be prepared for full report.

Nori sobered. She didn't want to think about going home. Not now.

Kiah came by early the next morning. Her flight was leaving nearly four hours before the U.S. departures, and she had to be at the airport by seven.

"Hooroo, mates," she said.

Amberly shook her head sleepily. "I never have any idea what you're saying."

"I'm saying good-bye, luv."

Nori saw her to the elevator.

Kiah handed her a slip of paper with her e-mail addy and cell number on it. "Keep in touch, would ya? And if you're ever in Oz…"

"Same," Nori said. "If you're ever in Ohio…"

"Doesn't that mean 'good morning'?" She winked.

The elevator arrived and swallowed her. Nori waved as the doors closed, then trudged back to the room, swiping away a stray tear. This was it. The end had begun.

The U.S. and European students prepared to leave in the next wave, around nine thirty. Nori was looking through the group, memorizing faces, when she noticed the tight cluster of Germans. Wait. Where was Erik?

She glanced around casually. And then she saw him. In the lobby. Standing apart from everyone else.

"What's with Erik?" she asked Amberly. "He forget to shower or something?"

Amberly's eyebrows shot up and her perfect little cupid's mouth tightened into a little *O*. "Didn't you hear?" she whispered. "No, of course you didn't. You and Atsushi were… out." Her eyes slid furtively left and right, and she leaned close. "He lost the scholarship. That presentation of his? Plagiarized. Every last word. He would have been sent home, too. You know, if we weren't already going."

Wow. Nori glanced back at Erik again. He stood alone, hands deep in his pockets, staring out the window. Hmmph. And he'd had the nerve to call her a liar! Nori tried to feel smug, but all she could muster was sorrow. Even after everything that had passed between them, she would never have wished this humiliation on him. Not in a million years.

She excused herself from Amberly and slipped inside.

"Erik." She touched his arm. "How are you doing?"

He jerked away and leveled a scathing glare at her. "Yes, this is what I would expect from you."

She blanched. "What are you talking about?"

His blue eyes flashed anger. "You should feel vindicated now. But that's not enough, is it? You have to come rub it in."

"No—"

"Not interested." With that, he turned on his heel and stalked away. Nori watched him go.

"Nori." Amberly leaned in through the open lobby door. "The bus is here."

"Coming." She looked around the lobby one last time. With a pang, she realized that she was going to miss it.

"Hey, Seaweed."

Nori spun around. Atsushi stood in the doorway. His khakis and Outreach blazer had been replaced with well-worn jeans and a faded T-shirt.

"You came," she said.

"You think I would miss saying good-bye?"

They walked outside together. "Yo, Amberly," he called. "Congratulations!"

Nori furrowed her brows, looking from one to the other.

"The scholarship," Atsushi said. "It was awarded to her. Didn't she tell you?"

Amberly blushed. "Well, I didn't want to make a big deal out of it."

"Oh, Amberly! But it is a big deal. Good for you!"

They talked about nothing as long as they could, but then Ms. Jameson bellowed, "Let's go, people. Everyone on board."

Atsushi helped Nori and Amberly load their suitcases into the cavernous space underneath.

"Well, I guess this is it." Nori reached out to shake Atsushi's hand.

He ignored her hand and pulled her into a hug instead. "Take care, Seaweed."

She didn't trust herself to say anything more, so she just nodded, pushed away, and followed Amberly onto the bus.

Atsushi stood until the bus pulled away, hand raised in farewell. Nori waved back, wondering if she would ever see him again. She fingered the *meishi* card in her pocket. Who knew what the future would bring? For now she would just have to be content with his friendship.

"I learn only to be content." Yeah. She got it now.

All the way to the airport, Nori felt a strange calm. Even when Amberly made her pose with the dork squad for a departing photograph. Even when the check-in line moved like molasses and they had to rush through customs to make their flight. Even when she sat on the plane, realizing how much she was going to miss Baba and Jiji and worry about Baba's health. And even when she thought of her parents and their problems waiting for her on the other end.

"Wasn't that the coolest thing you've ever done?" Amberly gushed. "I had the greatest time! Didn't you? Wasn't the food awesome? Can you believe I can eat rice with chopsticks? Oooh, hold on. Hottie alert. Don't look now, but three rows back…"

Nori listened to Amberly's monologue all the way 'til the first round of drinks and peanuts, and she didn't even roll her eyes once.

And when she drifted off to sleep in the middle of the flight, she could swear she'd caught a glimpse of that fifteenth stone.